DEATH MISCONSTRUED

A POISON INK MYSTERY

BETH BYERS

SUMMARY

May 1937

Georgette Dorothy Marsh has been revealed as the author Joseph Jones and she decides happiness is being away from the town she fictionalized. She's joined her friends in Bath and is enjoying the bookstores, the beautiful walks, and the teashops.

When she gets pulled into one book lover's crazy life, Georgette realizes that a murder has occurred. Now, it's a race against the killer as she tries to keep the book lover alive and find the murderer before the killer strikes closer to home.

For Carissa.
Thanks for saving my bacon yet again.

CHAPTER 1

GEORGETTE DOROTHY MARSH

To say that the goddess Atë adored Georgette Dorothy Marsh was to say a mother adored her only child. To say the goddess of mischief adored Georgette *more* after her status as the author Joseph Jones was revealed was entirely insufficient. It was, in fact, the great joy of the age for Atë.

"Georgette Marsh?" the bookseller asked. "Isn't that funny? Have you read that article about the person behind the Bard's Crook stories? You share the same name."

Georgette tucked a loose hair behind her ear as she glanced towards the ground and a slight blush crossed her too-white cheeks. Rapidly, she considered before she replied. "I did read that article. Funny, isn't it?"

Atë's impish gaze landed on Georgette once again as she filled her arms with books, and the most roguish idea occurred to the goddess. Her far-seeing gaze turned from the multi-faced Georgette and landed on the young, strong Harrison Parker. He was currently sitting with his Aunt Parker, telling her of his love for Georgette.

Atë's expression shifted to a smirk as she looked Parker over. He was tall, handsome, talented even. Arrogant and a bit baffled that the plain Miss Marsh had turned down his proposal. They were—in his opinion—perfect for each other. Barring Georgette's looks, of course.

From Harrison Parker, Atë turned her devilish expression to Charles Aaron working in his office. He was not, she thought, a man who would become accustomed to his good fortune. He'd bypassed many an opportunity to love. When he chose Georgette, it was *not* settling. It was what he'd always wanted encompassed in one package that was utterly enchanting to him—looks and all.

Despite all of that, Atë considered the layered favorite, Georgette, again. There, perhaps, happiness on either path that Atë laid before Georgette and how very fun would it be to see which she chose?

Georgette finished making her selections, adding to the pile on the counter in front of the bookseller. She glanced towards the front of the store and was shocked to her soul to see a display with *her* books. How had she missed *her* books on her voyage through the shop? Her stories were arranged in an appealing fashion with her Bard's Crook stories, the magazine that contained the article about who she was, and—in fact—a small chalkboard announcing the upcoming Bard's Crook story and her new unrelated novel, *Josephine.* The chalkboard offered to place an advance order for either of the next of Jones's books.

She crossed the bookstore and let her fingers trail over the spines. The blue linen covers, the silver embossed titles, the name she'd chosen for herself. It was all there. Georgette lifted a book and opened it, enjoying the crack of the spine being opened for the first time. Georgette sniffed deeply, taking in the fresh paper and ink smell of her book. As she let her fingers trail the words she wrote, she stared in a surreal shock.

It wasn't as though she'd never seen or touched her books before—of course she had. But not in the wild, so to speak. It was somehow impossible that Georgette watched as a woman crossed the bookstore, looked at the pile of books, glanced at Georgette, and then lifted the second volume of Bard's Crook for herself. Georgette stared with a wide gaze as the woman looked again at Georgette and back to the volume in her hands.

"You should buy it." The woman was older. Her hair was white, pulled back at the base of her neck. Her dress was simple, worn, and grey, and her

3

expression was one that Georgette had often seen in the mirror. There were worlds behind those brown eyes, but Georgette would wager the success of her next book that this woman was one who had been overlooked nearly as often as Georgette. A sister wallflower perhaps. One who, like Georgette, had been alone too often. So often, perhaps, that she ached for quietness too?

It was that very desire for aloneness that had Georgette leaving Mrs. Parker's home and venturing into Bath alone. Georgette had not realized the utter luxury of having a cottage to herself until she'd been packed like a sardine into a too small house with the Parker family for her visit with her dear friend, Marian. The room that was to have been Georgette's had been taken by Harrison Parker. Georgette and Marian were sharing a room and between them and their dogs, they were tripping over simply everything.

Georgette looked down at the book in her hands and took in the words she'd written under the watchful gaze of the woman. The black ink was so stark against the page. Georgette had written this scene on a rainy evening when she'd been hungry, but the cupboards had been mostly bare. She'd become accustomed to being a little hungry. She realized as she read her words over, that her character was hungry in the book. How often had she written her own feelings into the pages? How many times had she been tired and someone she'd written had gone to bed? What an odd world, Georgette thought, looking at her book and up to the woman again.

"Do you think so?" Georgette referred buying her book. She wanted to hear *why* the woman thought Georgette should buy it. A sort of undercover searching of compliments about her writing. A true review from a usual woman and not a professional reviewer.

"It is not every day that you can walk into a bookstore and buy a book you wrote," the woman told Georgette with the merest lift of an eyebrow.

"That I wrote?" Georgette looked behind her as if she'd find some fellow holding a sign that said this woman was the author, Joseph Jones.

The woman held out her hand. "Edna Williams. I overheard your conversation with Mr. Landry. I apologize for eavesdropping, but obviously, my dear, there are not that many Georgette Marshes. One who holds the book that woman wrote as though it were an unexpected prize? Elementary, my dear Miss Marsh."

Georgette took the woman's hand and admitted, "You've found me out so easily, Mrs. Williams."

"It's Miss," the woman said. "I wonder if I could further impose? I should very much like a pot of tea from the little shop across the way and I would adore speaking with someone who loves books like I do."

"Tea does sound lovely," Georgette answered, thinking of the crowded Parker house. The chance to chat over books? Perfection. "I should enjoy that very much."

"Mr. Landry," Miss Williams said, "do be a dear and have Miss Marsh's books delivered. I have captured her for tea."

The man laughed as he nodded. "Of course, Miss Williams."

Georgette was whisked out of the bookshop, having purchased her own books in the wild, and she followed the woman across the cobblestone street and into a little shop that seemed to have been attacked by crocheted lace doilies. The scent of the tea in the air lit Georgette's eyes with fire, and she bypassed the little table to the pots of loose tea in all their varieties.

"Oh!" Georgette said as she lifted a lid and took a deep breath. "Oh—" Her voice trailed off on a happy sigh.

"Do you enjoy tea, Miss Marsh?"

"I believe tea is one of the things that makes life worth living, Miss Williams."

"Try this one," Miss Williams said, tapping the top of one of the jars. Georgette opened the jar, breathed deeply, and ahhed. It was blackberry black tea, the scent reflecting a nice blend of both flavors. "Do you like the unusual teas?"

Georgette nodded almost frantically and Miss William tapped another jar at the very end of the counter.

"This one seems to have a hint of caramel," Georgette said. She had little doubt that her eyes were wide and excited, and she could feel she was flushed. She'd have been surprised to know, however, that Miss Williams was thinking that Miss Marsh was rather lovely, in a quiet sort of way.

"This is my favorite evening tea," Miss Williams said, nudging another canister. "Tastes a bit like a fruity merlot."

Georgette made a mental note to buy some of all of them and then joined Miss Williams at the table. To Georgette's utter delight, they simply spoke about books. Georgette's favorite, Jane Austen, was not quite as high for Miss Williams, who adored Anthony Trollope's Barset books. Georgette unequivocally adored some more ridiculous books like Edgar Rice Burroughs and V.V. Twinnings while Miss Williams tended towards afternoons reading John Donne and Shakespeare.

"What made you write books?" Miss Williams asked as their teapot was refilled and Georgette added an excess of milk and sugar to her teacup.

"Money," Georgette said simply. "Things were quite dire before Aaron & Luther purchased my book. Since then, they've been slowly looking up."

"Oh how lovely," Miss Williams said.

Georgette smiled as she asked, "What is it that you do with your time, Miss Williams?"

"I was a school teacher. I was able to retire recently when my cousin inherited a house here. She invited me to come stay with her and passed within six months, leaving me quite alone but not homeless."

"I am so sorry," Georgette told her.

"Thank you, dear," Miss Williams said. She started to say something when a gentleman came into the shop.

"Aunt Edna," the fellow said, "there you are! Is this the friend that is staying with you? Jane, isn't it?"

Georgette glanced at Edna, who gave Georgette a pleading look.

"Georgette," she answered, picking up on Edna's distress. "Though sometimes my friends call me Jane."

"That's a funny nickname," the man said, taking a chair from the table one over and helping himself to one of the small sandwiches on the plate in front of Georgette and Edna.

"There was an odd number of us at school," Georgette lied. "Jane was a joke that stuck."

"Funny," the fellow said, not looking amused in the least. "So you went to Aunt Edna's school and stayed in touch."

"She was very inspiring for me," Georgette told him without a trace of guilt and watched as Edna's worries deflated. "Corresponding with your aunt is one of the great blessings of my life."

The scoff that Edna's nephew didn't bother hiding irritated Georgette, but she'd long since discovered that being quiet and boring got rid of these fellows quicker than interacting with them. She smiled demurely, sipped her tea, and pondered on whether she wanted to start writing mysteries.

If she wrote detective stories, she could name

this man who hadn't introduced himself and then kill him off in her book. Or perhaps she'd write a new series called *Bath* that followed the exploits of the rude young man.

"This is my brother's son, Kaspar," Edna said, giving Georgette a relieved smile. "I told you about him. He sent me a wire saying he was coming down to visit and I had to apologize that my extra room had already been offered to you for the next month."

"Oh," Georgette said, her mind skipping ahead and wondering just how they would get out of this lie. "I'm so sorry to be in the way."

Kaspar did not reply but Edna said, "Darling, if I had known my dear nephew was coming, I would have been able to arrange things for him. He understands, of course."

Again Kaspar said nothing but he did feign a smile and take the last of their sandwiches.

"I'll see you at dinner then," Kaspar told them. "I look forward to getting to know you better, Jane."

Georgette didn't reply as Kaspar kissed his aunt's cheek, gave Georgette an unreadable look, and exited the teashop.

"Oh dear." Edna sipped her tea with a trembling hand. She looked to Georgette with wide eyes. "I am so very sorry, Miss Marsh. I had hoped he'd go back to London if I told him the room was taken."

"You had better call me Georgette," she replied, "or Jane if you prefer. Might I pry and ask what is going on?"

CHAPTER 2

GEORGETTE DOROTHY MARSH

Soon after her tea, Georgette returned to the little house that Mrs. Parker had taken. As she walked up the steps to the house, Marian exited with all four dogs on leashes and two envelopes in her free hand.

"Oh! I was hoping to find you," she said. "My goodness, Harrison spent the last two hours whining to me about how you didn't even tell him no when he proposed. That you just left him describing how great your life would be, the children you'd have, that he even agreed to let you keep the dogs—" Marian couldn't hold back her laugh. "Your version and then his—it was...it was... oh, I felt blessed indeed. I wrote it all out while he was talking to me and will be sending it off to Joseph."

"I told him no." Georgette leaned down to pet her loves, Susan, Dorcas, and Beatrice. Dorcas wriggled so fiercely, Georgette was forced to pick the dog up and accept her frantic kisses. The other two dogs were so offended that Georgette knelt on the sidewalk and gave all three of them—along with Marian's pup—loves until the chorus of whining died down. "Looking back, however, I am not convinced he proposed. I believe he just decided it would happen."

"That does sound like him," Marian said, clucking at the dogs until Georgette rose and took two of the leashes. "A bit cowardly really. Not even bothering to mention feelings or admit that he might not be the prize he thinks he is. Every woman deserves that question with a preface that begins with affection and ends with love."

Georgette led the way towards the little path they'd become accustomed to wandering together. Mrs. Parker was having dinner with friends in Bath whom she hadn't seen, and the rest of them had arranged to have dinner at one of the local restaurants, but there was still quite a bit of time before they needed to leave.

Marian handed Georgette a letter, and she realized she was blushing as she stared down at the precise writing of Charles Aaron. Unlike the previous letters, she realized, he had addressed this one himself. There was something so odd in feeling loved because Charles hadn't used his secretary to speak to her.

My Dearest Georgette,

Shall I tell you how much I hate that you are there while I am here? Or that I have spent the last two days in meetings with authors who have half your talent and not even a quarter of your agreeability?

The letter continued with an account of his days and ended, *"I find I cannot continue in London while you're in Bath. The stack up of my meetings over the last torturous days have freed me. I'll be on the train by the end of the week for a working visit to Bath while you're there. It seems that I have become worried that you'll succumb to the handsome Harrison or realize that you don't need me after all."*

"Oh," Georgette gasped, interrupting her reading. "Charles is coming!"

Marian grinned in a way that told her she'd already known.

"Is Joseph coming too?"

Marian nodded, a light blush on her cheeks. Her gaze flicked to the side, and her lips pressed together as if she had to hold in a reaction. "I've already sent Harrison over to secure rooms. I wrote it all out for the hotel as Joseph requested. Harrison doesn't know that Charles is coming. Dear, I didn't tell Harrison that you've promised yourself to Charles, but I do think you should reveal that little tidbit."

Georgette nodded absently, her gaze turning back to her letter.

I had no notion that succumbing to loving another left

one with an aching emptiness when the beloved was not near. I pray that you'll be as happy to see me as I will be to see you. I await your reply and the news from Eunice on locating a place for us to live so this insufferable separation will come to an end all the sooner and you'll be secured as my wife before Harrison succeeds in making you realize that he is young, talented, and handsome. I read his book as you requested, and you were right. After the changes you helped him see were necessary, it was quite good. There is a part of me that wishes to refer him to another publishing company, but I believe my partner would disown me if I did.

With my deepest affections, I look forward to your reply,

Charles

Georgette glanced up with a certain knowledge that Charles was coming. She had little doubt that her own cheeks had the same flush as Marian's. The two friends grinned at each other as they hooked arms to continue upon their walk. They bypassed a pretty little rose garden and the gate to a small park that had a few nursery-aged children out with their mothers or nannies, and then stepped onto the main road where Georgette intended to buy an excess of tea from the shop she'd visited earlier that day.

"Oy, Jane!"

Georgette didn't so much as look up because she'd heard her false name but because someone was hollering in the street. She turned towards the shouting, saw the nephew of Edna Williams, and then whispered to Marian. "Go with the lies."

"What?" she asked as Georgette turned and smiled.

"Why hello, Kaspar, fancy meeting you here."

"I wondered if you wanted to accompany me to my aunt's home?" He was, she only just realized, quite a handsome man, with a deep brown tan that set off his blue eyes and golden hair. He was perhaps around the same age as herself and Harrison.

"Oh that is nice," Georgette lied. "This is my friend, Miss Parker. I've arranged to spend the evening with her, but I imagine I'll be seeing you soon at dear Edna's." Georgette stumbled over the last word as she realized she had no idea if Edna lived in a house, a cottage, a set of rooms, or even a caravan.

"Indeed. Tea tomorrow, isn't it?" he asked and Georgette found herself helplessly nodding.

"Did you go to the same school as Jane?" Kaspar asked Marian as though there wasn't almost a decade between the two women.

"Ah, no," Marian replied. "We're friends…outside of school?" Although Marian was telling the truth, she was so bad at lying, it came out as a question and left her flushed.

"How do you know Jane?"

Marian looked frantically at Georgette, who said, "It is Georgette now that I'm not at school anymore."

"Of course," Kaspar said, his gaze landing on Georgette's face before looking at Marian again. Georgette could almost see him calculating the difference in their ages too late. He looked

14

awkwardly between them, cleared his throat, and then leaned down to pet the dogs.

Marian stared hard at Georgette while Kaspar's head was turned down but tried to blink it away when he stood.

"I'll be seeing you soon," he said, too intensely. His gaze landed first on the *lovely* Marian and then turned to Georgette. Given his frown, she wasn't sure that he believed his aunt's lie, but Georgette had no idea even *why* Edna Williams was so determined to keep her nephew out of her house and why she hadn't just said no.

"What in the world was that?" Marian breathed as Kaspar walked away.

"I don't even know," Georgette admitted. She described the afternoon with Edna Williams.

"You bought your own book?" Marian asked, completely ignoring the relevant information.

"I did," Georgette squeaked, and she put her hands over her mouth.

"They had a display?"

Georgette nodded, her lips pressed together to hold back the second squeak.

"And they have a tea shop here that you love? Maybe we should move to Bath."

In the same moment, both women shook their heads. Bath was too far from London. With Marian's fiancé a Scotland Yard detective and Charles owning half of a publishing company, they needed to find a village within a reasonable train ride from London.

"Perhaps we should just stay in London?"

Again, in unison, they shook their heads.

"What we need," Marian told Georgette, "is somewhere quirky like Bard's Crook, but where you haven't made an enemy of half the town."

Georgette scowled at Marian's smirk and then couldn't help but laugh. "I find that I feel very out of place in Bath. I don't know everyone."

"Neither do I," Marian said with twitching lips.

"Oh no," Georgette said, nudging Marian's arm. "Not all of us have traveled the world over and lived in the city of strangers."

"I like Bard's Crook, too. They're completely mad but lovable," Marian told Georgette. "When I imagine us married to Joseph and Charles with our little ones running around, I don't want to think of London's air in regards to my children, let alone neighbors who don't even know your name."

Georgette grinned. They were engaged to be married to an uncle and nephew. Though, Joseph Aaron was around Georgette's age, maybe a year or two older while Charles was a decade ahead of his nephew.

"Has Eunice found anywhere for us to live yet? My mother won't let me set a marriage date until after Joseph has somewhere to take me. His bachelor's rooms won't work."

Georgette shook her head. Eunice was technically Georgette's servant, but in practice, Eunice was family. She had taken on the task of packing Georgette's cottage and setting it up to be sold after Georgette had been revealed as the author, Joseph

Jones. Given that Georgette had fictionalized her neighbors' lives in her novel to the terrible result of multiple murders, Bard's Crook was no longer so welcoming of Georgette Dorothy Marsh.

They made their purchases from the tea shop with Georgette buying so many teas that she was going to have to double her intake or, she thought with a smile, share her teas with Charles. Eunice, darn the woman, refused to drink anything other than English breakfast tea or Earl Grey. Charles, however, had accepted Georgette's odd teas without a quibble and had even come to love the one with cocoa and coffee in it nearly as well as Georgette.

They were walking down the street slowly as neither of them really wanted to return to the house and Harrison.

"You will, though," Marian turned to Georgette, "tell Harrison that you're marrying Charles before he comes."

Georgette winced. Earlier that day, Harrison had left the snippet of his newest book and a rose next to her plate. He really seemed to think that he could just wear her down. There was a part of her that wanted to box his ears. There was a part of her that was flattered. The fact that those two parts of her were so diabolically opposed made Georgette wish to box her own ears.

"Yes," Georgette promised, ignoring the roiling anxiety in her stomach. "Of course I will. It would be unkind to let him discover that when Charles arrives."

"When will he be here?" Marian asked.

"He didn't give a specific date." Georgette nodded at the bookseller, who had just stepped outside of his shop and was locking the door. The day was coming to a close for the little shops. Georgette and Marian had been the last visitors to the teashop. "I think it's going to depend upon finishing things that need to be done in London."

Marian nodded, her mouth twisting, and Georgette had little doubt that her friend was wishing that Joseph could work as easily far from London as Charles could.

CHAPTER 3

CHARLES AARON

"When are you leaving?" Joseph asked as Charles loaded his briefcase later that same evening.

They hadn't discussed Charles leaving for Bath, but they'd both walked around the subject since they'd left Bard's Crook for London while their ladies had gone to Bath. No one had chosen Bath so much as followed Mrs. Parker, Marian's aunt, there.

Charles was, he supposed, grateful to Mrs. Parker for giving Georgette a place to stay while her cottage was being sold and they were searching for a married home. He was also selfish enough to wish that Mrs. Parker had been willing to take the ladies to London or even Mersea. Somewhere close enough to pop over for a day or the weekend.

Charles hadn't received a reply to his letter to Georgette, but he had little doubt that she'd welcome him coming to Bath when he arrived. He calculated quickly in his head and realized she'd probably only received his letter that day. Until they found somewhere to live, their marriage plans were paused.

Charles scowled as he considered. He'd thought it would be easy to find a place for both of them to live, but they were struggling to find a place in London when they wanted it for just a short time and Georgette finally said they should just find the village, buy the home, and marry. He didn't disagree that was the rational thing to do, he just disagreed on the delay.

He glanced at his desk, checking for anything he'd left behind while wondering if Georgette wanted a large wedding. They hadn't discussed it, but if he had to guess, he'd say that she'd be happier with a quiet wedding rather than attempting something large. Maybe she was assuming *he* wanted a large marriage? He didn't. It would be an avenue for those who were mere acquaintances to appear. Those who he really wanted there? His nephews. Perhaps his partner, though Luther wouldn't be offended if Charles were to elope. He'd just clap Charles on the back, wish him well, and hand over another author to handle. Luther preferred the handling of distribution and contracts while Charles discovered the writers and dealt with them directly.

"It's not clear yet," Charles told Joseph, noting the envy in his nephew's gaze. Charles grinned at his nephew and winked. "We've a bit more freedom than you and Marian. Is her family still eyeing you sideways?"

"As though I were going to run her off to Gretna Green or whatnot. Steal her away and refuse to bring her back."

Joseph's fiancé was watched far more closely than Georgette—who was entirely free to do as she wished. With a large dash of *protective* reserve, Joseph's future in-laws were welcoming. The reserve was more for the age difference than a dislike of Joseph specifically. Charles's nephew was thirty-one and Marian was only nineteen.

"You have no idea when you're leaving?" Joseph stretched his neck.

Charles paused in clearing his desk to examine his nephew's worried gaze. "It'll depend on when Micah Banister can come in for his meeting about his latest manuscript. He prefers not to meet with Luther, so I'll need to be here for that meeting before I can go."

Joseph nodded, distinctly uncaring of Charles's business concerns. Charles began packing his pipe before they left the office. He had been ready for a pipe for the last half of the day but too busy to stop and enjoy a smoke. If Joseph wanted to talk about *why* he was worried, Charles wouldn't be waiting any longer for that pipe.

Joseph watched as Charles put a match to his

pipe and lit a cigarette himself. "How goes the house and village search? Mr. and Mrs. Parker won't let Marian even set a date for our wedding until I've got a house for her. She wants a big event, so it's not like we'll be doing anything other than choosing something in the future and scheduling the church. I'm going to pin her down when I reach Bath regardless of her mother's wants. We can ensure we have a house before then, but it'll give her a chance to focus her attention on the wedding and get things moving."

"We're dealing with similar delays," Charles admitted. "Georgette *could* move into my rooms, but I realized we'd become packed to the gills when I looked for a place to put her things. *She'll* be happier, and I as well, if we start in a new house together. Especially as there isn't room for Eunice, and I have no desire to alienate her."

As far as his nephew's situation went, it was all too easy for Charles to see both sides of the issue. On Joseph's side, he was a respectable man with a good position and money in the bank to pay for his home. On Marian's parents' side, their daughter was very young and had fallen for the dashing, older man quite quickly. To Charles's surprise, he found himself thinking he'd be as protective of his daughter as the Parkers were being of Marian.

Charles patted Joseph on the shoulder. If the delay was not having a home, there was an indefinite one before them both.

"I sent Robert down to help Eunice finish with the cottage. They'll be done in a day or two and then Eunice will go over the lists of villages we've been sending her. Eunice will narrow down where to look, Georgette will find a likely village, and I'll come in and agree to whatever she says. You are determined to buy in the same village?"

Joseph nodded absently. "Marian won't forgive me if we don't. I'm convinced she loves me, but your Georgette is necessary to Marian's happiness, especially with her mother not being in the same village. We could stay in London, but Marian chose Georgette over her family already. If we live in London and you in Harper's Hollow or wherever you choose and then I have to travel? No, it won't do."

"Georgette does seem to nest in your heart until you'd prefer not to live without her," Charles agreed. "She also doesn't treat Marian like a child. I think that might be part of your problem with Marian's family."

Joseph nodded. "You think the girls are getting into trouble?"

Charles looked up in alarm. Why would his nephew even ask that? But he shook his head in answer. Of course they weren't. Georgette was responsible, Marian was a good girl. She might be a bit young, but she followed Georgette's example.

"Really?" Joseph asked, sounding surprised. "Not even a little bit of trouble?"

"I'd prefer to assume that they're drinking an

excess of tea, walking an excess of dogs, and generally reading an excess of novels. Georgette could do Aaron & Luther a favor and write another bestseller."

There was too long of a silence before Joseph agreed hesitatingly, "I'm sure they're doing all of that."

Charles glanced up again in alarm. "Why are you asking this?"

Joseph began to pace, stopping only often enough to drop his ashes into the ashtray.

"Think about those two," Joseph muttered as he paced. "Georgette wrote a very charming little book that had her neighbors murdering each other."

Charles puffed on his pipe. That was all too true. It had been pure madness but it was also when he'd realized she had captured his interest, imagination, and soon after his heart.

Almost manically, Joseph added, "*Then,* she wrote another very charming little book that was almost entirely fictional. Which caused two murders and a side of blackmail."

Charles winced and puffed heavily on his pipe until the clouds of smoke were rising over his head as though he were a train chuffing up a hill.

"Then, of course," Joseph said, "they were in Bard's Crook, which seems to be the quietest, sweetest little hamlet in the countryside of England. I'm not saying Bard's Crook isn't rife with mad people. Many places are. That being said, Bath is no hamlet. Given that it's far larger—"

"There are more mad people to find," Charles finished.

"Exactly," Joseph said tellingly.

"Still, it's hardly London," Charles protested, but his nephew's worry infected him. "Perhaps they're taking the waters? Visiting the bridges? What else is there to do? They don't know anyone there, by Jove!"

Joseph laughed. It was a sarcastic bark that chilled Charles.

"Perhaps they'll go for a swim," Charles suggested, sounding desperate.

"I'm sure they will go swimming," Joseph agreed darkly, "and stumble over some drowning victim."

Charles cleared his throat, shooting his nephew a quelling look.

Joseph snapped his mouth shut and let a few minutes pass before he asked, "Would you like to go to dinner?"

"Who can eat after the worries you've dumped on me?"

"You'll be in Bath soon," Joseph reminded him. "Let me know if there's trouble and I'll see what I can do."

Charles shook his head and tapped his pipe. Joseph had ruined whatever peace Charles had about Georgette being in Bath. It was bad enough that Harrison Parker was there *with* Georgette while Charles was in London working. That might even be worse, Charles thought. The man had, after all, wanted to marry Georgette.

Charles wasn't blind, so he knew that to most

25

people Georgette was nothing more than another quiet, plain spinster. Her pretty smile and bright eyes were there for anyone with wit to see but few did. Harrison Parker was not, however, stupid. He'd seen those pretty eyes and smile as easily as Charles had—eventually anyway. When you added in that Harrison had discovered Georgette's cleverness? It might just make Harrison appealing in return.

Charles loved Georgette for the way she looked through everything around her, catching glimpses of what most people missed. She didn't just see more deeply, which was fascinating in and of itself, but she took the little threads of interior lives and wove the details into new stories. It was enchanting.

Again, however, that wasn't why he had fallen in love with her, but he had to admit it was how she'd captured his imagination. He'd fallen in love with her because she was kind, thoughtful, and generous. His love was as simple as her unfettered kindness.

What if Harrison saw the same things in Georgette as Charles had? What if Harrison had gone beyond seeing a woman who could help him become a published author and realized she was actually a treasure?

"I've become a little girl," Charles told his nephew, taking a deep inhale of his pipe and then opening the door of his office. Dinner would be a distraction at least. "Harrison Parker is there, you know. Lurking, sharing the same house."

"He *did* propose to Georgette," Joseph told his uncle with a mischievous grin. It was the kind of grin that both took pleasure in the other's discomfort and yet—somehow—conveyed affection.

"You're riling up my worries to get me to go to Bath more quickly, aren't you?"

"They're trouble," Joseph told Charles. "Our girls are trouble magnets together and as we cannot talk ourselves out of loving them, we must instead try to keep someone from wringing their necks."

"Banister is not too far from Bath," Charles mused. "I wonder if he'd allow me to visit him in his home for this next meeting."

"Why wouldn't he?" Joseph asked as he hailed a black cab. "Then he doesn't have to rearrange his life."

Charles muttered options to himself aloud that would get him to Bath sooner. As he arranged the possibilities, Joseph admitted, "I cannot go this weekend as I had intended. I've got a case in Newcastle."

"Newcastle? Marian will be disappointed." Charles scowled at his nephew. "You deliberately worried me over them because you cannot go yourself."

Joseph's wince was nearly as deep Charles's had been when Joseph had been taunting his uncle about Harrison Parker.

"I might have done. But you'll go to Bath yourself, won't you?" Joseph asked, and this time there was a bit of a plea in it. "I'll check out that village, Harper's Hollow, on the way up to Newcastle."

"Deal," Charles agreed.

The two of them looked at each other and then shook their heads in unison.

"How the mighty have fallen," Joseph muttered.

Charles laughed and inhaled deeply on his pipe again. He was not, however, all that amused with himself.

CHAPTER 4

GEORGETTE DOROTHY MARSH

eorgette took a long deep breath in and then slowly let it out. Edna Williams's gaze was fixed pleadingly on Georgette in a way that she wasn't going to be able to say no to, but she knew better than to say yes.

"You want me to come to tea tomorrow?"

Edna hadn't let go of Georgette's gaze, begging with such utter entreaty that she was succumbing despite her good sense. Edna was a slender woman and her eyes were large in her narrow face, which maximized their capacity to beg.

Georgette had agreed to meet Edna only because Charles's letter had referenced delicious tea and it had occurred to her to send some to him. A sort of daily reminder that she wished he were here. Instead, however, Georgette's stomach was turning at what the woman was asking. The schoolgirl in Georgette wanted to please the 'teacher,' but her rational self reminded her hat she didn't have to comply.

"Please, dear?" Edna implored. Her eyes were starting to swim with tears and Georgette placed her hand over her heart to shield it, but it wasn't working. What was it about a woman asking Georgette for help? Was it because she had lost her own mother? Georgette's mother would have been of an age with Edna.

Thoughts of her mother had been on her mind since she'd left her mother's cottage, her grave, her friends, and the village she'd raised her only child in. Georgette had done so with a good riddance as far as the village and friends had gone, but she felt her heartstrings pull at leaving all remnants of her past and family behind.

"With my friends?" Georgette could just imagine explaining to the honest and stalwart Mrs. Parker that a short-term acquaintance wanted them all to come to her house, partake of her admittedly delicious tea, and lie through their teeth.

"Just for tea—"

"And lies?"

Edna winced, but she nodded gamely like a woman who knew what she wanted was irrational and wasn't afraid to want it all the same. There it was, Georgette thought, the difference between

Edna and Georgette's mother. Her mother would *never* have expected anyone to lie for her, *never* would have asked it of another, and would have been appalled by Georgette considering such a course of action.

"So you want me to bring my friends to your home, pretend to be this Jane, and lie to your nephew about staying with you and about who I am, all because you don't want your nephew who has taken time off work to see you to stay with you."

"Ah—" Edna winced but tried to hide it as she sipped the fabulous cherry marmalade black tea. "Please, dear. Just come to tea. Bring Marian and your Mrs. Parker. Are they any good at lying?"

Georgette shook her head and Edna laughed. "Well, we can't have everything can we?"

"But *why* don't you want your nephew to stay with you? Surely you can tell him that 'Jane' accepted an invitation to stay with friends when it was discovered that your nephew had arrived?"

Edna looked aside and blushed furiously before she said, "I am somewhat uncomfortable with gentlemen in the home. He's my nephew, but he's loud, somewhat smelly, and rather demanding."

The way she was blushing made Georgette certain that Edna Williams was not sharing the whole truth. Georgette had to wonder if there was any reason at all to help the woman.

Edna looked up at Georgette with tears in her eyes and Georgette slowly asked, "Why? Please, why? No prevaricating this time. If you want me to ask the very upright Mrs. Parker to lie to your nephew for you, I need to know why."

Georgette lifted her brows and Edna slowly said, "It's my cousin, Betty."

"The one who passed away?"

"She was quite fond of Kaspar, you know. He seemed quite fond of her as well, but the last time he visited before she died, they had quite the row. He stormed out furiously and while he was gone, she died. I—well, I suppose I'm being rather imaginative, but I can't quite shake the idea that something might have happened. That…that…caused her death."

Georgette shivered, staring at Edna, her mind skipping around like a rabbit being chased by a fox. There was something so terrible about looking at a woman who imagined that her nephew had killed her cousin.

"How did she die?" Georgette asked gently, taking Edna's hand. Georgette was attempting to be understanding. She could see how easily it would be for her to sum up the fears of this elderly, spinster, retired school teacher as nothing more than the fancies of an old woman.

Georgette, however, *despised* when mankind overlooked the plain and extraneous unnecessaries of life—like *herself* and Edna. Too often the single woman was seen as a silly idiot. And why? Merely because they were unmarried and childless.

"You think I'm a fool," Edna said, using the exact words that were necessary to sway Georgette to her side.

"You're not a fool," Georgette told Edna, completely uncertain of her statement. Perhaps Edna was foolish. Perhaps it was Georgette who was foolish.

"You don't understand," Edna said, ignoring Georgette's assurances and even the gentle hand that Georgette reached out with. "You don't know what it's like to be someone like me. How could you? A successful author, nice clothes. I was the teacher everyone disliked because I expected more than silliness and gossip from my students. Yet they all went beyond me, you know. They married and had children. Some found careers while I continue to be the foolish woman that no one believes when I say that dear Betty was murdered."

Georgette's mocking laugh paused Edna, who looked up in sheer shock that anyone would be so rude.

"I am the extraneous spinster of a small village who was descending slowly into utter and complete ruin. When I wrote *The Chronicles of Harper's Bend*, all I was looking for was enough money for bread and milk. I also do *not* consider someone marrying or having a flashy career as going beyond someone who lives a quieter or lonelier life."

"I don't understand," Edna replied.

Georgette stopped herself from rolling her eyes. "Yes, you do. Don't pretend to be silly when you aren't. You know as well as I do that a good number of those women who crowed about being married are miserable."

Edna paused, gaze wide, and she laughed. She shuffled a little and then straightened her shoulders as if she had to admit she'd been trapped by the truth Georgette gave the woman unequivocally.

"I understand exactly what it means," Georgette told her, "when no one even notices that you are around. It is, however, quite a leap to think your nephew murdered your cousin. You know that, it's why you avoided saying it. Uncomfortable with men? I hardly think that's the only reason you don't want him around. He isn't some random fellow, he's your nephew."

"So you think I'm wrong?" Edna's gaze was narrowed now, and she seemed almost offended, which bothered Georgette as well.

"I have no idea. Are you sure?"

Edna shook her head. "There will be others at tea," Edna said. "My friend, Mr. Osiris Page. I've invited my neighbors though I am not certain if they will come. The Allyn family is an excitable one and not in the fun way."

Georgette's head tilted as she asked, "What did the constables think happened to your cousin?"

"They said it was old age," Edna scoffed. "Old age that killed my cousin. She wasn't 90 years old. She was a vital woman with decades ahead of her."

"Was she of an age with you?"

Edna nodded and Georgette barely bit back her own scoff. Edna was certainly older than Georgette, but the woman wasn't so old you'd expect her to keel over for no reason.

"Was she healthy?"

"We went for long walks daily," Edna said. "She was healthy, active, and happy. No one would believe me because she'd had something of a sniffle in the weeks previous and it had lingered. They thought she'd just...just died from the complications of old age and a lung ailment."

"A sniffle?" Georgette demanded.

"A bit of a cough, a bit of a dripping nose, nothing that kills people."

Georgette immediately regretted what she said next. "People kill people."

"Exactly," Edna replied.

GEORGETTE CLOSED her eyes slowly and leaned back against the bedroom door she shared with Marian, who looked up from the writing desk on her lap. She was sitting on the bed, surrounded by a circle of dogs, all of whom lifted their heads, slapped their happy tails against the bed, and eyed Georgette as though she'd been gone for hours and hours.

"I have the worst favor to ask of you."

Marian glanced up from the letter she was writing. "You know I love you. I'll do whatever it is for free, but I do want to name a character in your next book. After me? Will you name the next Josephine after me? Because she's my favorite."

"Yes, if you'll help me convince your aunt to come to this tea that Edna wants us all to attend and lie that I'm Jane when I'm not because she's afraid her nephew killed her cousin."

Marian gasped at Georgette's rushed tirade. "I need you to repeat that."

"No, you don't," Georgette snapped. "She looked at me with these big eyes and I saw myself in her."

"You *are not* Edna Williams. You are not a foolish old woman who sees a murderer in her nephew. Really? Does she really believe that the fellow hurt his *own* aunt?"

"I feel like Edna Williams," Georgette admitted. "I feel like this life is all a lie and I'm supposed to be her. I'm supposed to be the one who thinks, my goodness, this is murder—and no one believes me. I couldn't say no. It would be like saying no to myself."

Marian put her pen aside and rose, taking Georgette's cheeks and squeezing them as if she were a baby. "You are not Edna Williams."

Georgette's eyes welled. "Does Charles really love me?"

Georgette knew she'd made a logic leap, but she had spent the walk back to the house thinking of Edna, herself, and Charles. What if she turned into someone like Edna and Charles regretted marrying her?

"You know the answer to that."

"I do." Georgette took in a deep breath. "I hate that my life feels like a dream. It feels like too big of a blessing. Why am I the one who falls in love—truly in love—when those like Edna are left alone and friendless? I'm having a difficult time enjoying my life because it feels like it should be someone else's and that's hardly fair."

Marian pressed her lips together. "It's not fair, but what's worse is how I'm going to have to hear about the tea where we lied to some poor fool for the rest of Aunt Parker's life. If Harrison goes to the tea, he'll bring it up every holiday we share. It's quite the sacrifice, you know?"

Georgette's eyes glinted with humor and Marian gasped.

"You like that idea. Me facing off with Harrison while he tells his pretty, vapid, attentive wife and children about that one visit to Bath where I—I—- got the upright, honest Aunt Parker to lie to a stranger."

"It's funny," Georgette said, not even bothering to hide her wicked grin. It wasn't just funny, it needed to be added to a book for the character Georgette named after Marian. That way Marian's family could pull out the book and show the younger generation the scene. A...a...word painting of that *one time* that Marian was wicked.

"Does it feel real now?" Marian countered with the corners of her mouth twitching. "Does torturing me feel real even when Charles feels like a fairy dream?"

Georgette's mouth twisted, and she refused to answer. "Come on then."

The two of them walked down to the parlor where Mrs. Parker was reading a book. She lowered it to greet them. "Hello, dears."

Georgette opened her mouth to ask the question and then paused. Marian was biting her bottom lip to hold in the laughter.

"Marian," Mrs. Parker asked, "why are you laughing?"

"Um," she said and giggled, wiping away a tear.

"Marian!"

She laughed, looked at her aunt, and then had to lean over to hold her side.

"Marian!"

"It's not her fault," Georgette told Mrs. Parker. "It's mine. I have the most horrible request."

Mrs. Parker reached out and cupped her cheek. "My dear girl, whatever I can do."

Marian burst into laughter.

"I—" Georgette couldn't say it. She gasped as she tried to say it, but she couldn't voice the request for Mrs. Parker to attend a tea and lie to strangers.

"Aunt Parker," Marian said while biting back her laughter. "Georgette needs you to pretend her name is Jane."

"No," Georgette said, gathering steam and courage. "My name is Georgette but people called me Jane in school, and you're supposed to know that. People call me Georgette now because I'm not replying to Jane for some random woman I met in a bookstore who recommended excellent tea."

Mrs. Parker stared. Her gaze moved between the younger women, noting their giggles, and the way they leaned on each other as they laughed. The dogs were at their feet, staring at the two young women with the same baffled expression that Mrs. Parker felt herself.

"So, I'm supposed to be staying with this woman I met at the bookstore whose name is Edna Williams."

"But you're staying here," Mrs. Parker told Georgette gently, as though she'd gone mad.

Marian's laughter was so loud they had to wait for her to finish.

Georgette nodded at Mrs. Parker when Marian's giggles faded off. "I am. I need you to lie. Well, she does. She's asked for our help, and I found I couldn't stay no."

"Lie?"

"Just a little," Georgette tried and then winced at the baffled, confused expression on Mrs. Parker's face. Georgette tried repeating, "Just a very, very little."

CHAPTER 5

GEORGETTE DOROTHY MARSH

Georgette found Harrison the next morning in the small breakfast room. He sat at the table with his manuscript before him, pressing his fingers to his temples as he read it once again in a low whisper. Each passage was said fervently, with a drama that few readers would ever imbue into his words.

Georgette had to admit, however, that he had taken every piece of advice, every suggestion, considered it, weighed it, and made changes. Even when he didn't take the advice Georgette gave, he at least took it seriously. He came to his own conclusions about whether there was an issue in his story, and he did his best to correct, clarify, and enrich.

"Harrison?" Georgette stepped into the room. She wanted to immediately turn around as she had done these last few days, but instead she forced herself to step in. They couldn't continue to live like this, and she had no idea when he was intending to return to his position. Even with that thought aside, Georgette and Marian were marrying an uncle and nephew and were good friends. There wasn't a scenario where Georgette would never see Harrison again.

Instead she crossed to the buffet and poured herself a cup of tea. She stirred in a heavy dose of milk and sugar and then sipped, barely keeping the scowl off of her face when she tasted the boring tea that Mrs. Parker served.

"Miss Marsh." Harrison looked up and smiled so sweetly she felt certain that she was about to crush him entirely. He did have a look of love in his gaze, and it did tug at her. She felt guilty for not loving him, but she didn't. She liked him. She admired him at times, but she did *not* love him.

She considered upon Charles, remembering the most enchanting list he'd once written. She'd taken to looking at the list he'd imagined for their life nearly every evening and she had—without shame—memorized it. There were, however, a few pieces that seemed to trot through her head anytime she found herself trying to think of something else.

-*Convince Georgette I love her.*

-*Convince Georgette to marry me*

-*Create a happily ever after?*

-Convince Georgette to share her troubles

Georgette would not have Charles arrive and find Harrison still imagining that he'd be able to persuade her to be his instead. Georgette would also not pretend that Harrison loved her. He didn't even see her. It was the very fact that Charles somehow saw into her heart that had persuaded her of his love. It was Charles's steadiness that had convinced her to trust him with her heart in return.

"I—"

Georgette stopped him. "I understand that you felt as though I was not fair in answering your marriage…" She would not use the word proposal, so it took her a moment before she was able to adjust it to, "declaration."

Harrison looked up with hope in his eyes and Georgette winced. "I cannot give you my heart, Harrison. It has been given to another."

"Another?" He sounded sick and Georgette shrunk inside. Yes, another.

"I am going to marry Charles Aaron," Georgette told Harrison evenly. "I am well aware of the kindness you have done me in wishing to have me as your wife, and I have no wish to disregard your affections callously."

"Etta—" Harrison begged.

"I cannot give you what you seek, but if you will accept it, I can give you my friendship."

His cheeks were burning as he cleared his throat. "I am well aware of the nature of such a gift, and I will accept it gladly." His words belied both his expression and his tone. Georgette winced again, feeling guilty once more for not loving him as he desired.

Georgette looked down at her tea, feeling sick, then slowly rose. "Your books are quite delightful."

His blushed deepened to such a level that Georgette was comforted. Her offer of friendship, her rejection of his love—none of it affected him nearly so much as complimenting his book. "Thank you. That means quite a lot coming from you."

She squeezed his hand as she told him, "I am merely one of the first to tell you so, Harrison."

"I sent my book to Mr. Aaron as you suggested," Harrison said, smiling once more at her, and squeezing her hand back. He squeezed rather too long, and she had to pull hard to retrieve it. "I addressed it to Robert Aaron also as you said."

Georgette listened to Harrison's monologue on his book until her mind had completely dulled, but he was distracted from the marriage offer, and she could stand to slap an attentive look on her face and pretend to care. Thankfully Marian entered the room soon after Georgette had refilled her teacup and suffered through another cup of boring but respectable tea.

"Hullo," Marian said, her gaze darting to Georgette before returning to her cousin. There was no question that Marian read the scene correctly. Georgette hid her sigh of relief, knowing that Marian would save Georgette from having to continue to listen to Harrison. "Did you write your letter? I was going to post mine this morning."

"I did," Georgette agreed. "A walk does sound nice." Escaping Harrison Parker sounded even better. Georgette paused with a flash of guilt for not inviting him before. "We're going to a very odd tea this afternoon, Harrison, if you'd like to go."

He agreed with a such hopeful expression that Georgette had to force herself to bite back a curse. Had he not completely understood that she was promised to Charles? Any guilt she had was swept away, replaced by a concern that she may have to repeat her refusal of him soon.

Marian grabbed the leashes from the cabinet near the front door and Georgette happily clipped them onto all four dogs. With a quick nod at Harrison, she jumped up and slipped out the front door before he could offer to accompany them.

"So you told him?"

Georgette nodded.

"How did he take it? Were you clear? That last look he gave as you invited him to the tea was enough to make me think you'd decided to throw Charles over for Harrison."

"No," Georgette told Marian.

"I'll still love you and think of you as a sister if you do."

Georgette wrapped her arm around her friend's waist. "I am not marrying Charles to be your aunt-in-law, hold you in affection though I do."

"Are you certain?"

Georgette said simply, "I never once expected a man to ask me to marry him. Let alone two."

"You have options," Marian told her. "Now that you're a famous author, you'll have more."

"You realize, of course, that isn't very appealing."

"Isn't it?"

"Now that I can take care of myself and make my life what I want it to be, I've discovered that the option of having multiple men offering for me is entirely unappealing. I used to dream of being saved, did you know?"

Marian shook her head, her gaze fixed on Georgette.

"I wanted a man to come along and offer me security. I wanted to belong to someone." Georgette was surprised by the burn in the back of her throat and her eyes.

"And?" Marian's quiet voice pulled Georgette from her memories.

"No one ever did."

"Did you cry?"

Georgette bit down on her lip. "Often."

"And then?"

"Then I stopped dreaming of it. I realized no one else would save me but me."

Georgette looked ahead down the cobblestone streets of Bath. The dogs were prancing along happily. It was as though Georgette were not, in fact, vomiting up the contents of her heart.

"So you saved yourself." Marian squeezed Georgette's arm tightly. "You're my hero, you know."

"I didn't just save myself and Eunice, you know," Georgette told Marian. "I learned how to be at peace with being the extra female. The one that no one wanted enough to see her for herself. I learned to like myself anyway and enjoy my own company. I learned all of it before I wrote my first book. The book wasn't the means to me liking myself—it was simply a way for me to pay our bills."

"So what do you want now?"

"I want to be loved, of course. For the person I am despite the fact that no one ever loved me back, beyond Eunice and my parents. That person isn't Harrison—who still doesn't see the real me, but I find myself surprised to truly believe it might be Charles."

They stopped at the teashop for tea worth drinking and then stopped again at a dress shop with the loveliest dresses. Georgette was arrested by the ivory lace dress in the window and knew, with utter certainty, that she might actually look lovely in the dress. With the cream lace and the scalloped edges and the way that it would emphasize her slim figure, Georgette thought it might even set off her skin.

What she wanted to do was ask Charles if they could bypass the big wedding, and perhaps even searching for houses, and simply get married. Perhaps her feelings made her seem something of a child, but happiness had been snatched away from Georgette so often that anything other than cherishing that which she'd found left her in fear.

"I want to try on the dress in the window," Georgette told the shop girl. The moment she saw herself in the mirror trifold, Georgette felt as though she were approaching loveliness. She spun in a circle, taking in the way her dress moved. She twisted to examine the crisscross of laces at the back, meant for decoration but lending an air of beauty found in the details of master craftsmanship.

She knew already she'd buy the dress, but she opened the door to the dressing room to show Marian all the same.

"Yes," Marian told Georgette instantly. "That is the one. With a little raspberry rouge on your cheeks and lips and your lashes darkened, your lovely pale skin will be emphasized."

Georgette glanced down at herself and felt pretty for the first time in her life. She'd gone from frumpy to passable to something else. Not truly beautiful but something a little better than average.

"Happiness looks good on you," Marian told Georgette.

Georgette paid for her dress with a smile before gathering up the dogs with Marian from the front of the shop. They walked slowly back to Mrs. Parker's house.

"My aunt is coming," Marian said as they approached the right street, "to the lying tea. She has decided she wants to see you be Jane and is thinking of it as playacting. Aunt Parker has added, however, that it's disgraceful that a woman of a certain age must lie to keep her unwanted nephew out of her house."

Georgette flinched. The invitation had been sent to them all, but she'd been hoping that no one but Marian would accept.

"Did you tell her why Edna doesn't want her nephew in the house?"

Marian shook her head. "I did write to Joseph about it, but I mentioned her circumstances. How she was older and single and somehow convinced you to pretend to be this fake student from her past. She sounds a bit silly."

Georgette tried not to flinch, given how heavily she identified with Edna Williams. Instead Georgette just said, "She could be wrong about her nephew killing her cousin and still have good reason to believe what she does. Her cousin did die and it did seem like she was a healthy woman, given what Edna said."

Marian glanced at Georgette. "You think she might be right."

"I think she's easy to overlook and that is something that I understand all too well."

CHAPTER 6

CHARLES AARON

$\mathcal{H}$e was going to reach Swindon momentarily, have his meeting, and find Georgette just after tea or thereabouts. He had a solid bet that she'd already discovered the best place to have tea. To be honest, he was craving her odd tea with coffee and cocoa and hoped she'd either brought her supply or knew where to get some. Along with, he thought, a layer cake. His love had taken to indulging often in cake. The result being that Charles also was wanting to indulge often.

Charles approved in the way her cheeks had gone from hollow to round. He approved in the way the light in her eyes shone more often, and the ridiculous indulgences she enjoyed more than anyone else simply because she had been denied them for so long.

The meeting took far too long and Charles nearly missed the last train to Bath. He had to run for it. Dodging through a line of children who had been lined up by their schoolteachers, their disgusted gasps had him flinching. He leapt on at the last minute and then cursed when he realized he was, in fact, going to miss tea. Charles reached the train car and saw that it was full. Surely the last train to Bath should be nearly empty, but it seemed the universe was frowning on Charles today.

He shrugged and found a place to open his briefcase. The more work he did while Georgette was enjoying her tea, the more chance he'd have to enjoy her company before he was dragged back to London.

When he considered London, he frowned fiercely. He could blame Joseph for his own worrisome thoughts, but it wasn't his nephew's fault. Had his nephew's worries extended to Charles? Yes. But he didn't want to go back to London without Georgette because of his nebulous jealousy or worries for her safety. He wasn't arrogant enough to assume she couldn't navigate her life without him. She'd reached her third decade without his assistance, and he had little doubt she could continue on her own. The truth was, he worried because he loved her. The truth also was, he didn't want to leave her behind because he missed her. He wanted nothing more than to elope and bring her home.

Was it wrong of him to ask her to set aside the kind of wedding that Marian was planning and elope with him? He wanted to ask her, but he didn't want her to say yes simply because he had asked. He wanted her to say yes because she'd also rather be together than separate.

With a sigh, Charles reminded himself that they'd be home together soon enough and the delay wasn't going to ruin him. Not working, however, just might. He opened the manuscript in front of him and told himself to focus on the words on the page.

GEORGETTE DOROTHY MARSH

Edna William's house was nicer than Georgette expected for a retired girls school teacher. Edna had inherited better than Georgette would have expected given their meeting. The house wasn't a mansion, but it was charming, with big windows, lovely furniture, and books that lined nearly every wall.

Georgette smiled as she introduced Mrs. Parker, Harrison, and Marian to Edna and then to Edna's friend, Osiris Page. He nodded charmingly, commenting on the weather before turning the conversation easily from one subject to another until he found one that interested Mrs. Parker and Edna both.

His gaze darted to Mrs. Parker over and over

again before he started to ask her if they had known each other before. Despite her denials, he ran through option after option until finally Mrs. Parker said he might have known her cousin, who Mrs. Parker claimed was very similar.

Georgette slipped to the side until Kaspar Williams entered the room along with the teacart. He glanced about and his gaze narrowed, lingering on Georgette for so long that she was sure he had discovered the truth.

"Hullo, hullo, Jane. How is your visit going?"

Georgette smiled up at Kaspar. "It is Georgette, you know."

Kaspar lifted his brow mockingly and he glanced about. "Look at all the friends you have in Bath. You're a fortunate one, aren't you?"

She didn't bother to answer.

Harrison turned to her charmingly. "I rather like Jane. Or Joseph. Even Josephine."

Georgette shot him a silencing look, but he simply grinned. Harrison's gaze was lingering again, and Georgette wanted to scold him. She'd helped him get his book to a publishing company, thinking that would be the end of his infatuation, but he lingered too long, as though he had to prove his feelings were connected to more than just his work.

"How funny you should say that." Kaspar glanced between Georgette and Harrison Parker. "I was just reading an article of my aunt's about this author named Georgette something or other who wrote under the name Joseph. I suppose she chose a man's name because it gives her book a better chance. Like George Eliot, you know. Women can't make it on their own."

In fact, Georgette had chosen a man's name to put another layer between herself and the discovery of her actual identity.

Harrison stared with a slowly dawning delighted expression, but Georgette squeezed his arm and shook her head very slightly. He closed his mouth but then his head tilted as he said to Kaspar, "You know, of course, that there are many great women writers."

Kaspar shrugged. "I think they're talented *despite* being female. There's a reason why there are so many male writers and so few female writers."

Georgette kept an even expression as she asked, "You don't think that the reason there are less female writers in history is simply because they were not educated? That generations upon generations of women were looked at only for their value as chattel and wombs?"

Kaspar laughed and dismissed Georgette as he addressed Harrison. "Perhaps it's because they're so emotional?"

Harrison held up his hands. "I happen to agree with Georgette."

"Have you read that Joseph Jones's book?" Kaspar scoffed. "We should have guessed it was written by a woman the moment we read the trite scenarios."

"I have read it," Harrison shot back, "and I quite liked it."

"What else have you read lately?" Georgette asked Harrison, hoping to avoid further talk of her own books. She already felt like a liar, but to be a liar quite so dramatically was making her extremely uncomfortable. "I've been traversing the Hercule Poirot mysteries."

Had she selected one of the greatest female writers of all time on purpose? Yes, the answer was yes.

"You know," Marian said, "I just read a book by Edith Wharton. It was delightful."

"Oh, how fun," Georgette shot back. "Ethan Frome?"

Marian nodded. "Just so wonderful. I may give it a few days and read it again."

"I didn't like that one quite as much as I liked Pearl Buck's *The Good Earth*. I have my copy with me, if you'd like to borrow it."

Kaspar held up his hands in surrender, but it was too late. Excellent books written by women were not rare because of the sex of the writers, and the sheer idea was offensive. The cheek! Georgette had traversed from disliking him mildly to intensely. She feigned a smile and then accepted the cup of tea Edna brought with a true grin and sat to enjoy it. It had that hint of caramel that Edna had suggested in the tea shop and Georgette closed her eyes in joy. She was going to buy so much of this tea that she'd need a suitcase to bring it with her to wherever she went next. The idea that she wouldn't be returning to Bard's Crook hit her all of the sudden, and she had to sip her milky sweet tea to hide a sudden sadness.

On her second greedy cup, heavy with milk and sugar, Georgette turned to ask Edna a question but there was a woman's screech from the street outside.

"Oh," Georgette squeaked, jumping and spilling tea on her dress. If she had been wearing the dress she'd bought for her wedding, she'd have wept.

The screech was followed by another and then a third as everyone in the room went silent.

"Oh dear," Edna said, leaping up.

"Surely you've heard screaming from the neighbors before?" Kaspar asked. "That Anna Allyn is a handful. Her poor husband."

Georgette faced Kaspar. "Perhaps it's poor Anna."

"You think that sounds rational?"

Georgette scowled at him. "Do you have any idea what kind of husband he is? Do you know him personally?"

Kaspar shook his head. "I suppose I know details but they're all from my Aunt Betty and now Edna."

Georgette didn't let up. "I think that you cannot possibly know the horror a woman knows when she has a cruel, unkind, or terrible husband."

He held up his hands again in surrender and Georgette looked to Edna, who rose and said, "Sometimes she just needs a word."

Edna stepped out of the room as Mr. Page crossed to Georgette. "It's all right, my dear. Mrs. Allyn is a handful, but she calms down rather quickly when Edna talks to her. I wonder what they did before our Edna moved closer. Our poor Betty wasn't nearly so gentle with Anna as Edna is."

Georgette set aside manners as she rose and crossed to the window. Mrs. Allyn was a woman so beautiful that she made every other woman—even the very pretty ones—feel as plain as Georgette.

Mrs. Parker seemed nearly as alarmed as the woman in the street. "My heavens," Mrs. Parker said when the woman threw something glass onto the street outside. If Georgette were to guess, she'd assume she was seeing the destruction of wedding china.

Edna hurried down the porch stairs of the small house with a spryness and lightness of foot that surprised Georgette. She watched as Edna simply opened her arms and the young Mrs. Allyn threw herself in them.

"Oh!" Marian said. "I love her. Look at that—"

Anna pulled back and said something to Edna. None of them could hear what was being said between the two women, but there was so much tenderness there that Georgette felt herself fighting sympathy tears.

"Aunt Edna is the kind of wonderful that gives you hope in all of mankind," Kaspar replied. "Aunt Betty as well, though differently, from Edna."

Harrison glanced towards Kaspar. "Given your recent comments, I wouldn't have thought you'd say that."

Kaspar looked between the friends. "I don't

dislike women. I might think they are not as mentally smart as men, but I do think women are far smarter in the heart. Aunt Edna, Aunt Betty—they might not speak Latin, but they make life better. They observe things those of us who have education miss."

Georgette looked through the window once more. Mrs. Allyn was weeping in Edna's arms.

"Is Mrs. Allyn's life truly awful?" Georgette asked quietly.

"I wouldn't want to be married to her husband," Mr. Page answered.

"Why?"

"He has a second family."

Georgette gasped. "And Mrs. Allyn knows?"

Mr. Page nodded. "She's left him twice, but he convinces her to return every time. If not for his sons, I'm not so sure Mr. Allyn would bother."

"And you described *her* as irrational?" Georgette accused Kaspar, who had the good sense to look abashed. She turned back to the window. Mrs. Allyn's golden hair was pulled back with a black headband. Her dress was black as well with a red belt around her waist. She wore black stockings with seams up her legs. "Look at her. She's everything every woman wants to be, and she's not enough for him? No wonder she's irrational and emotional. You would be too."

Anna Allyn's lips were full, her cheekbones high, and her eyes large, but she was too far away to see the color. Georgette had little doubt that Mrs. Allyn had brilliantly colored eyes that were the jewels of her face.

"The secrets Edna probably knows from all those street-side hugs." Kaspar shook his head. "She's a vault of state secrets."

When Edna returned to the parlor where she had her tea, Kaspar crossed and kissed Edna on the cheek. "Brilliantly done. You're a gem."

Mr. Page also crossed and whispered something into Edna's ear and she blushed deeply. Her gaze flicked to him and then back to the floor. Georgette knew that look, she thought. It was the look of someone who was baffled by the affection of another. She didn't miss that Mr. Page placed his hand over the top of Edna's.

CHAPTER 7

GEORGETTE DOROTHY MARSH

*A*fter the tea, Georgette, Marian and Harrsion sent Mrs. Parker back in a black cab so they could walk through Bath.

"Pulteney Bridge, I want to walk over it," Marian said as she walked next to Harrison, her hand on his arm. "I hope to go with Joseph when he comes."

"He'll come," Georgette told Marian from Harrison's other side. "Don't sound so mopey."

"It's unbecoming," Harrison told Marian, who smacked his arm.

"Oh look," Marian said, letting go of Harrison's arm to cross to an English bulldog. She dropped down on her knees to say hello to the dog. The fat old fellow wagged his tail as though it hurt to move it, but he was excited, and when Marian leaned down to accept his kisses, he moaned to her.

"Not you?" Harrison asked while they watched Marian accept the dog's kisses.

Georgette winced at the slobber and started digging through her handbag for a handkerchief for Marian. She pulled it out from under a book, a notebook and pencil for book notes, and Charles's letter that Georgette wanted to read for the fifth time before the day ended. If Harrison weren't with Georgette and Marian, Georgette would lean against the side of the bridge, unfold her letter, and savor it before daring to discuss dreams of the future with her dearest friend.

"I only like my own dogs."

Harrison's head cocked as he examined her. "You're funny, Georgette Marsh. I was convinced I had ruined my proposal when I said they needed to go."

"You did," Georgette told him plainly. The fact that he'd told her they would marry and declared she would have to get rid of her dogs infuriated her still. As though Georgette would ever let Susan, Dorcas, or Beatrice go. They provided her a daily, constant comfort, and were—in fact—part of Georgette's family. "I would have said no regardless."

"Because you love Charles Aaron?"

Georgette nodded. Charles, the dogs, the assumption that she should be grateful for his attention. She knew she wasn't all that desirable to the vast majority of mankind, but she still liked herself well enough to know she deserved better than such nonsense.

"Georgette?"

She turned from Harrison, her heart leaping. There he was. Distinguished in a fine suit, with kind eyes and a blank expression.

"Charles—"

His face was a mask, and she felt suddenly like she'd been doing something wrong. She hadn't, she'd been thinking of him in each passing moment, but if she'd come across him arm-in-arm with another woman, she'd have been hurt too.

"Charles!" Marian said, rising from where she'd knelt by the dog. "We were just talking about you coming and walking with Georgette on the bridge. You will, won't you?"

Bless Marian's perfect heart, Georgette thought. Her dearest friend knew just what to say to fix everything without even trying.

Charles nodded, relaxing just enough, and Georgette hastily dropped Harrison's arm and crossed to Charles. They stared at each other awkwardly and Georgette felt guilty again for no reason whatsoever.

"I—" She bit her bottom lip before daring to push up on her toes and kiss his cheek. "I missed you. I'm so glad you're here."

Charles pressed his forehead against hers and she closed her eyes, feeling the relief of his presence. At some point her home had shifted from Bard's Crook to him, and she hadn't realized it until that moment.

When they looked up from each other, Charles

confessed, "Joseph is concerned that you and Marian have gotten into trouble. Oh! I have a letter for her from Joseph."

Georgette paused and followed Charles's gaze. It seemed that they'd been abandoned. "Maybe they didn't want to be here when I told you about the last few days."

Charles's gaze widened. "What have you done?"

Georgette laughed at the expression on Charles's face and told him. "I will free you from my troubles, if you need it."

His expression was distinctly unamused.

Georgette put her hand on Charles's arm and they walked while she told him what she'd been up to. From seeing her books in the bookstore, to meeting Edna, to the request to pretend to be Jane, and somehow convincing Mrs. Parker to join in.

When she finished her tale, Charles asked, "Only Edna Williams realized you were Joseph Jones?"

Georgette nodded, shaking her head. She really would have thought that someone who bought a half-dozen books and shared the name with the recently outed author Joseph Jones would have—at the least—been asked if they were one and the same. Her persona was too quiet, too solemn, and too unassuming to be anything other than any village's spinster.

"Even with your name and the article? Georgette Marsh is not that common of a name."

She shrugged. She didn't understand it either and couldn't account for it.

Charles shook his head and then pressed a kiss against the side of hers. "Mrs. Parker lied?"

Georgette nodded, holding back the laugh. "Mostly she didn't say anything when the subject came up. Edna was better at deflection than I'd have thought. She jumped in and changed the subject every time."

Charles laughed. "I might call you Jane now."

"I prefer Georgette, Georgie, or even 'Hey You.'"

"What about Mrs. Aaron?"

She paused for a moment. "I've already agreed to that." Oh yes, she thought, that was *exactly* what she wanted. She wanted to curl herself up in his arms, take his name, and be each other's family. Each other's refuge.

"I wondered if you'd consider eloping as soon as we find a place to live. Be Mrs. Aaron sooner." His expression was fixed on her face, and she could see that he hesitated. He hadn't wanted to ask her even though he'd described exactly what she wanted.

"You don't want a big wedding?"

Charles turned her to him. "I want what you want, Georgette. But my choice would be together sooner."

"I want Marian, Eunice, Joseph, and Robert there."

"Of course." His gaze was searching hers. "This is what you want?"

"I'd rather have something small with those who are happy for us than anything else. All I want is to be your wife."

Charles pressed a kiss against her forehead. "I was so worried about asking you. I didn't want to take any dreams away."

Georgette adored his kind eyes. They were fixed on her face with the same expression that had convinced her that he really loved her—truly her and only her. "I want the same thing. A quiet moment between you and me for our wedding. That's all I want. I was trying to find a way to say the same thing."

"Eunice is checking villages and Joseph is visiting Harper's Hollow. If it works, what do you think? He swore to write immediately about the village."

"If the village has what we want," Georgette said, "surely we can find something we can live in? I'm not picky, I don't think. We could just go and see for ourselves."

"I don't know about just trusting what they say either." Charles hesitated and she could see the business reasoning come out in him. She was all instinct, and he balanced her with reason. "You're right. Let's visit ourselves. We don't have anything tying us to Bath other than each other. Why don't we take an auto for the day, have a picnic, wander the village like spies and see if it has what we want? Make sure it's the right place for us."

"Like spies? Sounds delightful."

"What are you looking for?"

"What feels right." She didn't know how to describe it. She wanted to go there and feel like she did when Charles appeared out of nowhere like he had that night. As though things had slipped into place.

"What feels right?" He pressed another kiss to the top of her head as though he needed to remind himself that she was truly with him. "If it feels right to you, I'm sure that the rest will work for me."

She laughed and then took his hand and tugged him after her. "Your reason is coming into play, and here I am talking about what feels right. Do you feel as though you've dipped into fairyland? Or just straight madness?"

"I think that what feels right to you is based off of little things that you notice and add up with your instincts. It isn't madness. Maybe, I'll just follow your instincts instead of my reasoning."

"I think you give me credit I don't deserve."

He just shook his head.

"How are we going to know we found the right place? This feels like such a big decision. I'm not sure I'm prepared. It's the rest of our lives. What if we mess up?"

"How can we?"

Her laugh was a scoff. How could they mess up? She'd written a simple duo of books and caused death and mayhem.

Charles tugged her back to his side and slid his hand around her waist. "This is only our beginning. Eventually, we'll be settled in our house. We'll make it our own, the combination of both of us, and it'll feel like we should never have lived anywhere else or been apart at all."

Georgette pressed her blushing face into his chest. "You're the one who should be writing books, not me. You know just what to say to make me feel like we can't possibly go amiss."

"We can't, Georgette, when we've decided upon happiness, no matter what little bumps might appear in our path. If I wanted simple, I'd have remained a bachelor."

They were making their way through Bath without any plan when they found Anna Allyn storming down the road. Georgette whispered to Charles about the evening. She told him of the breaking china, the crying in Edna's arms, and the declaration from Mr. Page that Mr. Allyn kept a mistress and had additional children with her.

"How did I miss a story about a tantrum in the street?"

"You weren't paying attention," retorted Georgette.

Charles teased before admitting, "I was distracted by the rest."

Georgette tugged on his hand, so she could follow Anna Allyn. The woman's looks were only highlighted by her fury. She moved as though each step was an assault, her hands fisted at her side, and her expression said she'd storm the castle and retrieve the princess. Dragon or no dragon, this was a woman who intended to conquer.

Georgette was distracted from her observations by Charles who cleared his throat before saying, "So, let me get this correct. Edna Williams thinks her nephew might have killed her cousin."

Georgette nodded. It sounded less ridiculous when the woman was begging for someone to believe her with wide, sad eyes.

Charles hadn't experienced the same, but he only said, "She somehow convinced you to make her nephew believe that you're staying at her house, so she doesn't have to have the potential murderer in her home."

Georgette nodded and Charles's gaze moved over her face with the weight of a caress. It was a loving look, but a baffled one, and he asked, "How?"

Georgette pressed her cheek against his shoulder. "I saw myself in her."

"You don't see yourself correctly." Charles sounded affectionate, but still baffled. He lifted her face to his and pressed a kiss against it. "You are not what you think you are."

"What if you are wrong, not me?" she shot back.

"I'm not," he said, kissing her forehead again. Mrs. Allyn had turned, and they moseyed after as though they were randomly ending in the same location as the woman. The fact that Charles didn't question it was one of the reasons Georgette adored him.

"Wait until Joseph hears that there was talk of another murder. He will come down here, throw Marian over his shoulder, and drag her before a priest despite the protests of his in-laws."

Georgette put off Charles's attempt to lighten her

mood. "I can't decide if I believe her or if I think she's ridiculous."

Charles's hand squeezed her waist, and Georgette barely hid a jump. She had gone so long without being touched by anyone at all that she wanted to both purr like a cat and flinch away. Instead of doing either, she pulled Charles to a stop and wrapped her arms around his waist, hugging him tightly to her.

"You are going to have to be patient with me while I learn how to, well, everything."

"Everyone is going to remind us how we're set in our ways."

"What if we are?"

"What if the reason we found each other is because we fit?"

"Can you stand if I jump sometimes when you touch me?"

"Can you stand the smell of pipe smoke?"

"I suppose I could get used to it."

"Then I can as well."

She grinned at him and then told herself to relax against his chest. They were shooting questions and worried at each other with a speed that left her dazed and feeling a little exposed.

"What about breakfast?" he asked. "What do you eat?"

"Tea and toast or tea and buns. You?"

"Poached eggs and bacon."

Georgette scrunched her nose. "As long as I can have tea. I can handle the scent of bacon when my stomach would prefer to be sleeping."

"You can have toast as well," he said magnanimously.

"I write in the night sometimes," she said, testing him.

"I'll endeavor to tire you out."

Georgette flushed so brilliantly that Charles laughed and pressed another kiss on her forehead. She buried her face against his chest again. "I didn't realize it would be so hard."

Charles's head tilted in question.

"I thought saying yes would be the hardest part. As much as I want to be with you, this is all terrifying."

Charles rubbed his chin against the top of her forehead. Before he could find words for her, some comforting promise, they heard Anna Allyn shriek. Both of their heads turned and they found Mrs. Allyn staring at another woman.

The second woman was pale, thin, and she had spots on her chin. She was also heavily pregnant with two little girls in tow. She appeared not to notice Mrs. Allyn as she continued on her way, but Georgette saw the second woman's gaze flit to Mrs. Allyn a few times as she hurried the little ones along faster.

"Oh no." Georgette eyes widened as she watched Mrs. Allyn shake her head frantically before turning to run. The conquerer was gone and a broken woman was left behind. Before Georgette could stop herself she pulled away from Charles to reach out toward the fleeing woman. "Mrs. Allyn?"

Anna Allyn stopped and stared at Georgette. Georgette might have been an utter stranger, but she knew what it was like to feel like nothing.

Mrs. Allyn hesitated.

"I'm a friend of Edna Williams," Georgette told her. "Please, can I help?" She reached out her hand in an offer of comfort. The woman blinked rapidly and then threw herself into Georgette's arms.

Georgette was quite shocked—they were strangers, after all—but she hid it as she held the younger woman.

"I don't understand," Mrs. Allyn whispered. There was an accent there and it took Georgette a moment to realize that Mrs. Allyn was Australian. No wonder she let her husband talk her into coming back again and again. She may not have anyone to provide her refuge. "I don't understand why he does this to me. Why did he promise me forever? Love? Is this being cherished?"

"No," Georgette said, crying with Mrs. Allyn. "No, of course it isn't."

"Edna said she'd give me the money to leave."

Georgette tried to prevent a gasp, but she wasn't quite successful.

"I—" Mrs. Allyn pulled back and then sniffed, taking the handkerchief that Charles provided. "I'm sorry. I have to go."

CHAPTER 8

GEORGETTE DOROTHY MARSH

"How do we avoid that?" Georgette asked Charles as they watched the weeping Mrs. Allyn flee.

"We could start by my not having a second woman in my life."

Georgette's daggered glance had him stepping back.

"I feel like I just had a flash of what will happen when I make you angry."

"*When?*"

Charles chuckled and pulled her back to his side. It was as though they needed to wrap themselves up in each other after seeing what happened when love went wrong. "I feel it's inevitable that I'll infuriate you. I suppose it's even inevitable that you might cry."

"I cry reading books," Georgette said, but she was haunted by Mrs. Allyn.

"I have little doubt that things will go wrong between us from time to time. But I'll be damned if I ever see you as broken as Mrs. Allyn."

Georgette closed her eyes. "It's safer, isn't it?" she asked tonelessly. "I could buy a little cottage and live a boring, lonely life."

"Please don't." The pleading in his voice had her opening her eyes, and the look on his face was enough to confirm that not only could she trust him, but the idea that she might leave him would wound him terribly.

"I don't want to be safe alone," she told him, offering him the same reassurance he had just given her. "Not anymore. Whatever happiness I could have harvested from that kind of life is gone for me. I'm not sure I can ever find it again."

He clasped her to him and they stood in silence, sharing the sense of belonging and acceptance between them.

Charles drew away to look at her. Though she was comforted at the moment they'd shared, her worry for Mrs. Allyn crept upon her once more.

"I want to make sure that Edna checks on Mrs. Allyn," she told Charles, who answered with a simple nod.

Charles looked nearly as worried as Georgette felt as they followed the direction Mrs. Allyn had gone. He hurried her along after the poor woman. As they reached Edna's house, they saw Mr. Page leaving. He crossed to them calling, "Jane!"

Charles choked back a laugh as Georgette said, "Why hello, Mr. Page. May I present my fiancé, Mr. Charles Aaron? Charles, this is Edna's good friend, Mr. Osiris Page." Introducing Charles as her fiancé gave her a tremble of joy.

The two gentlemen shook hands. Mr. Page faced Georgette. "I wasn't aware you were engaged, Miss Marsh. In fact, poor Edna hoped that you might find something to appreciate in Kaspar."

Georgette flinched at the thought and had to wonder if Edna ever told the truth at all. She could hardly expect Georgette to find anything of interest in a nephew that Edna accused of being a murderer. Why would she build that lie? What purpose could it possibly serve? Georgette checked Charles's expression, which was bland, and then said quietly, "I believe that any connection between myself and Mr. Williams was an idle fantasy on Edna's part."

Mr. Page nodded, his gaze heavy on the two of them before he said, "I should go. It was very nice to meet you both."

Georgette stared after Mr. Page before leading Charles towards Edna's door. "What an odd lie to tell Mr. Page."

"Indeed. This is the murdering nephew?"

"Or, she's a very odd liar."

"There is something about you, Georgette. With Marian, you were nearly instant friends. With Mrs.

Allyn, she threw herself into your arms. With this Edna, perhaps she dragged you into her oddness when she realized you were a willing audience."

Georgette pulled Charles after her and knocked on the door. She considered what Mrs. Allyn had said about Edna giving her the money to return home. Could Edna afford to send Mrs. Allyn and her children, if she had any, to Australia? The woman was a retired school teacher not an heiress. Unless it was all another lie she'd told to Mrs. Allyn.

No, Edna had seemed truly upset over Mrs. Allyn's state. Perhaps, Georgette thought, Edna had inherited money from her cousin.

What if Kaspar had thought he was the heir so he murdered his aunt only to discover that the money had been left to Edna instead? Would he be working on weaseling his way into Edna's will?

Georgette shook her head. Edna's troubles were done for Georgette. She was going to find a village with Charles, elope in the dress she'd purchased, and find a way to be happier with him than she was alone. First, however, Anna Allyn.

Edna opened the door. Her eyes widened when she saw Georgette and Charles. "This is a surprise."

"We met Anna Allyn," Georgette told Edna before the woman could say anything more. She searched Edna's face. "She needs someone to check on her. I believe she just discovered her husband has a child on the way with another woman." It was the only explanation for Mrs. Allyn's reaction to the other woman.

"Oh!" Edna muttered, "I was hoping she wouldn't find out."

"You *knew?*"

"Everyone who knows them knows. It would have been easier for her to choose to go home than to be driven home."

Georgette didn't agree in the least. It would have been far easier for Anna Allyn to find out from a gentle friend, with a cup of tea, and a shoulder to cry on. Georgette discovered she was enraged that Edna had left Anna alone in that situation. Georgette was, in fact, enraged in general.

"I'm done being Jane, Edna."

"Oh, well." Edna teared up, but Georgette had just seen Mrs. Allyn fall apart. There was no comparison.

"I can't go on like this. I'm sorry."

"Of course," Edna said, blinking away a tear. "It wasn't fair of me to ask you."

"I'm sorry," Georgette said again lamely.

"It's all right, my dear. Of course it is. You did far more than you should have. I'm the one who should apologize. The tears—don't feel bad." Edna reached out and took Georgette's hand. "I've had the oddest day. These tears—" Edna shook her head and sniffled again. "They're not your fault. None of this is your fault. I've had such a shock. I just—" She shook her head and then kissed Georgette's cheek. "I'll take care of Mrs. Allyn. I hope I might see you again before you leave."

Georgette agreed, glancing at Charles, and said her goodbyes to Edna before she got sucked back into Edna's madness. Together, they made their escape.

"She's odd," Georgette said.

"She is odd," Charles agreed fervently. "I didn't expect tears."

"I think I might have," Georgette told him. "Honestly, I'm not sure anything she did would have surprised me."

They headed back towards Mrs. Parker's house, and Charles told her, "I think you might need to learn to say no."

She noticed the gleam in his kind eyes, and he glanced about and pulled her into the shadow of an alley, tilted her face towards him to rub their noses together until she laughed.

"I thought you were going to kiss me."

His eyes crinkled with those perfect laugh lines. "I just wanted you to stop feeling guilty first."

She laughed at the look on his face but then gasped as he put his arm around her and pulled her tightly to him. Before she could say anything, he took her mouth and she found that all the worries she'd had since she left Bard's Crook faded, as did all of Bath.

She had to catch her breath a few minutes later and hide her blush, once again, in his chest. This time, she realized that the feel of being touched by the man who loved her made all the fears she'd carried fade into nothing.

Charles cleared his throat, holding her against him until she shifted, and he stepped back.

"Harper's Hollow tomorrow?"

Georgette nodded. They walked slowly again, neither of them really wanting to return to Mrs. Parker's home. Georgette was craving something more from her life than sharing a room with Marian and not even having space to write.

"Let's," Georgette said. "Let's go, let's love it, and let's find a house."

CHARLES ARRIVED with the auto as the sun rose. Georgette and Marian were waiting with a basket full of food and picnic blankets. He seated them both, and they started on the road. Motoring across England was something of a gift. What Georgette realized as they drove, however, was that she loved Marian more than anything—except Charles. Georgette would have happily left her friend at a train station and spent the day with Charles alone.

She wasn't sure that anything could give her more comfort about the choice she'd made than to realize that Marian—the one friend who had been an incessant comfort to Georgette—wasn't as comforting as Charles. Georgette took in a long breath and let it out. She needed that understanding more than she could have known. She'd needed to know that Charles loved her, and he'd been convincing her of it with each passing day.

She'd been worried about the more physical side of marriage, and those fears were fading. She'd been worried that being with someone so much would suffocate her, and she was discovering the opposite.

Harper's Hollow rolled out before them between two hills and a flood of trees. There a small square at the center of the village that housed a beautiful church, a gorgeous bank with pillars and grey stone, and a bridge that arched over a small, quiet river.

The river begged to be rowed. The bridge begged to be explored. The trees, in the distance, begged to be climbed if Georgette were younger. Next to Charles, however, she could imagine children climbing them. The thought of children, her children, in this village—it was overwhelming.

"Yes," she told Charles.

He grinned at her. "I know we brought a picnic, but the pub—"

"Let's try it," she grinned, glancing at Marian, who had a wide gaze fixed on the river.

"I can imagine many a Saturday afternoon on that river."

"As can I," Charles agreed. "I have already decided to buy a rowboat."

Georgette stared about her. "Does this feel like a dream to you?"

"Yes," Marian said instantly. "I thought that Harper's Hollow couldn't be better than Bard's Crook, but look at this place."

They ordered fish and chips in the pub and Charles ordered a pint. The fish was flaky and golden, delicious in every way. The chips were crisp and satisfying and the fish was flakey with the batter fried to perfection. Georgette looked at the other two and then took in a deep breath.

When she'd sold her first book and brought home cake for herself and Eunice, it had felt surreal. She hadn't realized you could find joy and take care of the people you loved at the same time.

When Charles had proposed and she'd found the faith to believe in him, it hadn't seemed possible that she was even living the life she was living. But now, in this village? If they found the right place to live, it would be as though she'd been given too big of a blessing. It was unfair, especially when she considered people like Mrs. Allyn or Edna Williams. Georgette took another deep breath in and held it, secretly biting the inside of her mouth.

Before they drove out of the village, they decided to circle it. They didn't have much time to make it back to Bath before it was far into the night, but, all the same, Georgette gasped.

"Stop the car!"

Charles hit the brakes so hard, they slid in the seats and Marian squealed before nearly landing on the floorboards of the car.

"What?" Charles asked, breathless, but Georgette was already outside of the auto. There on a little wooden plaque was a "For Sale" sign.

She grinned at him and darted past the gate. Three steps in and she had to stop. The house was close to gothic. She trailed forward, wondering if her eyes were deceiving her. The garden had monstrous oak trees that were interspersed with stretches of grass and an occasional weeping willow.

The house had to be at least three stories. Perhaps five if you counted cellars and an attic. The windows were dark and dirty, but the framing on them was arched in a half circle above wide, tall rectangles.

"What a dump," Marian said from behind Georgette

She gasped and turned, hand over her heart.

"Oh no," Marian told Charles. "She likes it."

"I love it!"

"Georgette," Charles said gently. "That window is boarded over. Who knows what vermin have taken up residence."

Georgette had already started moving again. She was at the side of the wall, pushing up on her toes to peek into the grimy window, but she said over her shoulder, "They have men for that."

"The roof needs replacing," Charles said almost desperately.

"Look at the garden again," Georgette ordered as he placed his hands on her waist and lifted her, so they both could see through the dirt.

The library door was hanging off its hinges, but the walls were lined with floor to ceiling book-shelves and a rolling ladder.

"The entire thing will need to be repaired, repainted and repapered."

Georgette didn't answer. She could see her books lining those walls, interspersed with Charles's. She'd seen his rooms. The library might not be enough between the two of them.

"Then we can pick out everything."

"Darling," Charles groaned, "this house would drain us of everything we have set aside and leave us paupers."

"What if I write twice as much for the next year?" She knew she was pleading, but she loved this place. It was as though she'd come home.

"What if I'd like a scrap of your attention on occasion?"

"What if the vermin won't leave?" Marian demanded.

"Can't you imagine our children running in this garden?" Georgette demanded of Marian.

"It's overgrown," Marian answered.

"That can be fixed."

"Her eyes are even wider now," Marian told Charles. "She loves it more. What was on the other side of the window? An office for writers?"

"A library," Charles muttered.

Marian groaned while Georgette put her hands on her hips and declared, "It just needs some love and—and—elbow grease."

"Oh my goodness, she's never going to stop dreaming of this place." Marian stared around, shaking her head. "It is a neat old house, I'll give you that. It was probably amazing in its day."

"It's perfect," Georgette answered.

"It's got good bones, I suppose," Charles admitted. "The gate needs replacing. The roof. The paint and possibly significantly more. For the right price—with double books—maybe? I don't know, Georgette."

She smiled gently. "It feels right."

He didn't miss her reminder of their earlier conversation.

"You haven't even seen the inside," he argued reasonably.

"I don't need to." She trusted her instincts.

"This is what comes from loving an artist instead of a...of a..." Charles wasn't able to come up with an alternative.

But Marian did. "A school marm."

Georgette spun in a circle, closing her eyes and letting the feel of the house flow over her along with the warmth of the sun, the wind, and the people she loved with her. "I love it."

"Let's be reasonable," Charles told her. "We'll see what the price is, but we can't overpay. Not with all the work it needs."

He took her hand. "We really do need to get back on the road. I'll send Robert or my secretary over to discover who owns it, but don't get your hopes up, Georgette."

"Too late," Marian answered.

Georgette didn't reply at all. She was too busy arranging everything in her mind.

CHAPTER 9

When Atë's far-reaching, impish gaze followed the auto through the curving roads of England, she grinned. Her delighted grin always had an edge of wickedness and that wickedness was emphasized as she considered their thoughts. Each of them was thinking of the village, Harper's Hollow, but they didn't know what she did. They were silent as their thoughts traveled different roads.

Charles was imagining his letter to Joseph explaining Edna's theories about a murder and the way Georgette had been pulled in. Which, of course, pulled in Marian and would send his poor nephew spiraling. It had been an easy thing for him to escape with the ladies to look at the village, try the pub, and say yes. He liked Harper's Hollow. For Charles, all he needed was easy access to a train to London and for Georgette to be happy.

Marian was thinking about Joseph and how he was so far away. She had been completely and utterly jealous of Georgette that day, wandering with Charles and able to envision their future together. At the same time, however, while her beloved had been gone—she hadn't been alone. It would have been so easy to be alone without Georgette. Marian had glanced into the front seat where Georgette and Charles had tangled their fingers together and known that even as often as Joseph had to travel, she'd never be alone.

Georgette, however, was thinking of that house. She wasn't entirely irrational, so she knew it would be a headache to turn that disaster into a home. And yet...how did you balance what was rational with what felt right? The willow trees, the massive oaks, the stonework that proclaimed care and thoughtfulness in building the house. The big windows where the sunlight, combined with the shadows of the trees, would enter and form delightful patterns on the floors.

She was still thinking of the house when they arrived back in Bath. Charles stopped the auto outside of Mrs. Parker's house when it was nearly 9:00 p.m. They were all sore from bouncing over the roads and the long motoring across England. Georgette's back ached, her neck was sore, and she wanted a long soak in a bathtub with Epson salts.

As they got out of the auto and packed up their

things from the drive, Mr. Osiris Page walked down the front steps.

"What in the world?" Marian breathed as they nodded to the man.

"How was Harper's Hollow?" he asked genially. "I must say, I enjoyed taking your place at dinner."

"Harper's Hollow was lovely," Marian told him. "We adored it."

"I'm sure your aunt will miss you when you move there."

Marian laughed and shook her head. "Oh I doubt it. She's moving closer to grandchildren, and we'll see her often enough. She'll be glad to get rid of me."

"Her grandchildren?" Mr. Page asked. "I assumed she'd stay here."

"Oh no," Marian told him. "She's just selling her home in Bard's Crook and finding one near her daughter. This is a stopgap since dear Aunt Parker doesn't want to share a home with her daughter. They're both, ah, strong-minded women."

"Well," Mr. Page said, "you're all lucky to have such a woman leading your family."

Georgette glanced at Charles and found she wasn't able to hold back a yawn. He nodded and excused them, ignoring Mr. Page's desire to keep chatting.

"He's probably a lonely old man," Marian said with a look to Mr. Page, who was walking alone down the sidewalk towards the main road just beyond. "Desperate for friends and attention."

As Marian stepped inside, Charles whispered,

"Don't get your hopes up, Georgette. It would take everything falling perfectly into place for that house to work out."

Before she could reply, Harrison stepped into the hall.

"You've got a card from Mrs. Williams," Harrison said. His gaze moved between Georgette, Marian, and Charles. "I believe, given what the boy who delivered it said, you've been invited to come rather early tomorrow."

Charles groaned while Georgette opened the letter and skimmed it quickly. "She wants me to come so she can express her gratitude."

"Just you?" Marian asked.

Georgette nodded.

"No," Charles said. "She's not right, Georgette. I suppose it's paranoia, but after the last few months, I'm not sure I have that much trust left in me. I wouldn't feel comfortable for you to be there alone."

Georgette's mouth twisted as she considered. "We could go together, or I'll write her a note. If you don't want me to go, I won't."

"Either is fine with me," Charles told her.

"Let's go see what she really wants," Georgette told him, and a bit of her inner mischievousness flashed across her face. "What good fodder seeing her will be for my next book."

"We need to get you somewhere where you can write," he told her. "Or we might have to move back to Bard's Crook and live in your little cottage."

"Surely you can write here," Harrison said. "It's not like we don't have pens and paper."

Georgette shot him a glance and then turned back to Charles, very much wanting to take the room reserved for Joseph and escape this house. "Now that I've begun writing with a typewriter," Georgette explained, "it's rather hard to think using a pen. I've become spoiled."

She kissed Charles's cheek and disappeared upstairs before Harrison could say anything else. She was very much finished living with Harrison and Mrs. Parker. As much as Georgette appreciated them sharing the house, she wanted to leave.

She found Marian had already taken the bath when Georgette reached the bedroom. With a sigh, she sat down on the floor and stretched towards her toes. Her mind wouldn't leave the wonder of that house alone, and she curled up onto the bed with a pencil, a notebook, and ideas for the house.

She fell asleep on top of the paper while Marian was still in the bath and didn't wake until after Marian got up the next morning and the dogs wriggled their way up to Georgette's head. Beatrice licked Georgette's nose. She tried pulling the blanket over her head but Marian called, "Charles is coming, remember. Breakfast then Edna's house."

Georgette hauled herself out of bed, soaked her aches away, and stumbled through breakfast despite Charles's presence and a cup of tea. She didn't quite wake up until she took in a deep breath of air.

"Georgette," Charles said and gestured with a

single nod before they turned down a connecting street. She followed his gaze to Osiris Page, who was wearing quite a fancy suit, carrying roses in his hand.

Georgette gasped. "He couldn't possibly be romancing Mrs. Parker, could he?"

"Oh, I think he is," Charles told her. His kind eyes focused on Mr. Page. "They're not too old to love."

Georgette elbowed Charles lightly. "I wasn't thinking *that*. Hello, my darling Charles, I've spent much of the last decade being a spinster. What I was thinking was that they've spent so little time together. They should be discussing favorite books and what they like to do on Boxing Day. It's too fast."

"They have less time," Charles said, kissing the side of Georgette's face. "Rather like us."

"We're ancient," Georgette laughed.

"Decrepit." Charles lifted her hand and kissed her knuckles. "We should savor every second."

Georgette laughed and they enjoyed the remainder of their walk in silence. When they reached Edna's street, both of them stopped as they saw Kaspar stumbling out of the house. He took in them and called, "Help! Help me, please. Oh help, help!"

Charles let go of Georgette's hand and pelted down the street with Georgette only paces behind him. They reached Kaspar and he moaned, "Doctor! We need a doctor!"

"Doesn't your aunt have a telephone?"

Kaspar shook his head and Georgette darted past

and up the steps to Anna Allyn's house. She banged on the door until a swollen-eyed Anna opened it. Two little boys were sitting on the steps behind her and Georgette noted the hall filled with trunks. She ignored all of that and demanded, "Do you have a telephone?"

Anna nodded.

"Call for a doctor. There's an emergency."

Charles stepped up to the doorway and added, "Put in a request for the constables. Edna is asking for them."

Anna hurried to make the telephone call while Georgette turned to Charles. Her gaze met his and she saw the worry in his eyes.

"Is she going to make it?"

"It's not good, Georgette." The look on his face said it was very bad indeed.

Anna watched them as she spoke into the telephone. When she replaced the receiver, she asked, "What's happening?"

"Edna Williams is ill." Georgette had no idea if Edna was *ill* or *injured*. Edna's theories about a previous murder were heavy on Georgette's mind as she considered the *healthy yesterday* woman needing the hospital today and asking for constables.

Anna's gaze darted to her children and she ordered, "To the garden. I'll be right back."

She ran out of the door and Georgette and Charles hurried after. They found Kaspar holding Edna's hand at the base of the stairs. It was clear that Edna had fallen down the stairs from her position. Her breathing was rough and her eyes were terrified. Terrified, but confused. Her arm looked broken as did her collarbone if Georgette was any judge.

"No." Georgette pressed her face into Charles's shoulder. She couldn't help but think back to Ruth Dogger the poor woman Georgette had found poisoned. Georgette had stayed with the woman while she wondered if she was going to die, and Georgette didn't want to do it again.

"Charles," Georgette whispered, "she looks so scared. She thinks someone was trying to hurt her."

"I know, darling," he said against the top of her head. There wasn't anything they could do other than watch until help arrived.

It didn't take long, and Edna was yet alive when she was taken to the hospital. What could they do for her? Would she make it? Georgette couldn't imagine how terrifying it must be for the poor woman.

"What happened?" Charles asked Kaspar.

"I don't know." He was swallowing over and over again. "I came by to tell her I needed to go back to London. I found her like that and I knew—that wasn't normal. Edna is light on her feet. She was a girls school swim teacher, did you know? She still swims often. She moves like a woman half her age. It didn't look like a heart attack and then falling down the stairs. It didn't look like a brain fever and then falling down the stairs. I don't understand what's happening. What happened to her? I suppose she could have tripped, but why would she be afraid of me if she had?"

Charles didn't answer and neither did Georgette, but both of them were wondering if Edna hadn't been pushed.

"Were you here when your Aunt Betty died?" Georgette asked.

Kaspar shook his head. "No one was. Aunt Betty was alone. Aunt Edna had taken a walk with Mr. Page. He'd come by, had tea with them both. Why?"

Charles didn't answer the question. "Tell us more, please."

Kaspar wasn't stupid, so he was following the same thought process that Georgette and Charles has already traversed. "You think that someone killed Aunt Betty?"

"Edna thought you did something to Betty," Anna told Kaspar from where she stood in the doorway. "She assumed you thought you'd inherit from Betty and you killed her to get the money."

"Me?" Kaspar shook his head and then muttered, "Women."

Anna glanced at Georgette. "It's why Edna lied about Jane staying with her."

"I realized that was a lie almost immediately." Kaspar pressed his thumb to his chest. "I just thought Aunt Edna was nervous around men."

"Do you think Betty was murdered?" Georgette asked Kaspar flatly, but she included Anna in the question.

"I hadn't thought so." Kaspar sounded doubtful.

"What about you?" Charles asked Anna.

She paused before answering. "I always thought that Betty was too healthy to have just keeled over, but the doctor seemed convinced, and what good did it do to encourage Edna's fears?"

Charles bit back the curse that Georgette was also swallowing. What good did it do? It might have saved Edna from sharing the same fate.

CHAPTER 10

GEORGETTE DOROTHY MARSH

"Now why are you all here?" A constable glanced around, shaking his head. "Why did you call for the police? Our time isn't to be wasted for little ladies who trip down the stairs."

Charles cleared his throat and started to explain their worries. Given the disbelieving and baffled look on the constable's face, Georgette had *little* doubt that they would make no headway.

In fact, Georgette thought, if she or Mrs. Allyn were the ones who explained why they were concerned about what happened to Edna Williams, they'd have been mocked immediately. Every time Charles referred to anything that Edna worried over or anything that Georgette had noticed, the constable snuffled, wiped his nose, and cleared his throat. The handkerchief was not a very good disguise for the mocking grin, and Georgette only just prevented herself from scolding the man thoroughly.

No wonder poor Edna had turned to a random woman in the bookshop for help rather than the constables. Charles, unlike Edna, got the benefit of being listened to—which wasn't much of an improvement.

"So let me get this straight," the constable said to Charles. "An old lady died in her sleep six months ago and you decide that this *other* older woman falling down the stairs is now an attempted murder? You realize that doesn't make sense, correct? Are you just listening to the worries of the ladies and pushing off on me having to tell them they're being imaginative?"

He turned to Georgette and Mrs. Allyn. "No need to worry, ladies," he said in a patronizing tone. "There isn't some crazed killer. Mrs. Williams just stumbled and fell down the stairs."

Georgette rose and walked away from the constable. It turned out that being the seen female was, in many ways, worse than being the unseen one.

"Miss, where are you going?"

"I'm feeling faint," Georgette lied and then left before he could stop her. She walked up the stairs of the house and opened door after door until she found Edna's bedroom. It was not the master bedroom, and Georgette guessed that Edna hadn't been comfortable moving into her cousin's room after her death.

Edna's bedroom was lovely with blue curtains and carpet. Silver-pinstriped blue paper lined the walls. The bed was a mess with the covers shoved back. Georgette noted every other aspect of the room was neat. The books were lined on the shelves precisely along the edge. There was no dress hanging over the back of the chair. Georgette opened the wardrobe and found that each dress was hung facing the same direction, with shoes that were paired, cleaned, and carefully placed in a row.

Georgette turned back to the bed. There was a pillow on the floor that looked like it had been tossed from the bed. It looked unseemly to the extreme compared to the preciseness of the rest of the room. She just couldn't see a person who kept their bedroom this neat allowing her pillow to lie on the floor. And leave the bed unmade.

What if someone used that pillow for nefarious reasons? What if the reason that the cousin, Betty, didn't wake from her nap was the same? Would anyone have realized that an older woman with a cold had been smothered if there were no signs?

What if the person thought they had murdered Edna, left her, and she'd survived and been disoriented? She might have fallen down the stairs then.

Georgette heard Charles call her name and she knew she needed to leave. If someone *had* tried to kill Edna, and the constables didn't think she was in danger, would the killer strike again at the hospital?

Georgette shivered and hurried down the stairs. The constable was waiting to lock up Edna's house while she was in the hospital, and the others were standing on the sidewalk. Anna's children had joined her and she was holding each one by the hand.

Georgette joined the others

"He didn't believe us at all," Kaspar whispered. "We're not foolish women or drunkards. Why—"

"Excuse me," Anna Allyn hissed, covering her older child's ears. "Your aunt was the woman who recognized what happened to Betty. Not you. Not the constable. The girls school teacher."

"Indeed." Georgette wanted to rush to check on Edna, but another idea was occurring to her instead. She met Charles's gaze and nodded away from the house. He understood and they left Anna Allyn and Kaspar Williams behind.

She told Charles what she had seen and then finished with, "Charles, I think we need to make sure that Edna isn't left alone until she's able to tell us what happened."

Charles didn't disagree, but his frown was deep and his gaze was distant.

Georgette didn't want to ask, but she was sure that he was concerned, either for her, or perhaps *them*. He had good reason to be, she had to admit, given all they'd experienced at Bard's Crook. Every so often on their walk back to the Parker house, he rubbed his thumb over her wrist or absently lifted her hand and kissed her knuckles.

When they walked up the steps, Georgette heard her dogs bark a happy greeting. There was a shout for quiet, and for a moment, she thought Harrison Parker was yelling at her dogs. A second later, however, Charles muttered, "Thank heaven." At her look, he added, "Joseph has arrived."

"Oh!" Georgette grinned at him. "Perhaps we can get him to speak to these local constables."

"Perhaps," Charles said, sounding unconvinced.

She considered for a moment and then realized that the local police would hardly welcome some London detective stepping in to tell them they were doing things wrong. Her mouth twisted and she sighed. That wasn't going to work. Unless—

She grinned and went into the house.

The parlor contained Mrs. Parker, Marian, Harrison, and Joseph. Upon a more careful study, she that found Robert Aaron, Charles's other nephew, had also arrived. They'd have been a crowded bunch in the small Bath house even without Mr. Osiris Page, but he had a prominent seat near the fire.

"There you are!" Joseph said. "How was your visit with Georgette's newest acquisition? I am unsurprised, Georgette, that you made friends so quickly."

"There was an accident," Charles said bluntly.

The gasps drowned out everything else. Georgette crossed to Marian to share her chair and greet the dogs. While everyone hung on to Charles's recounting of the 'accident,' he kept the details vague and only about Edna herself.

"How is her nephew doing?" Mr. Page asked, "losing his aunt like this?"

"The doctors haven't lost hope," Georgette told him. "It is hard, I know, to face losing another friend after Betty, but Edna is quite active and healthy. She may have untold reserves. Don't give up, Mr. Page."

He nodded quickly, gazing down at his hands where they were clenched fiercely. "You're right. First Betty, now Edna. It's hard for those like us, isn't it, Mrs. Parker?"

Marian's aunt jumped at the question. "Other than my dear husband, who died quite young, I haven't faced losing my friends yet. I pray it won't happen for some time."

Mr. Page nodded, glancing back down at his hands. "I suppose I am leaping to all sorts of conclusions today. I think I had better go check on Kaspar. At a time like this, he needs his friends."

After the door closed behind him, Charles turned to Joseph. "If it was an accident, I am a cuckoo."

Joseph's gaze met his uncle's and then he cursed.

Mrs. Parker moaned. "Not again. I am not doing this again, Marian. And neither are you or Harrison. Georgette, you should come with us. I suppose you're family now, and I won't see my girls embroiled or hurt because of some...some...fiend."

Georgette stared at Mrs. Parker with her kind face and ready acceptance. There was a fierceness there that declared Georgette one of Mrs. Parker's ducklings. Georgette had wished for nothing more than to be wanted by someone, and it was happening for her because of Charles and Marian. Georgette's eyes were, therefore, burning with emotion, as was her nose and the back of her throat.

"I can't tell you what that means to me, Mrs. Parker."

"It's Aunt Parker now." Her kind eyes softened despite Georgette's shaking head.

"I can't leave Edna alone."

"You're not responsible for her," Aunt Parker told Georgette. "She's a mature woman."

"Who was nearly murdered, I think," Georgette said quietly. "She's nearly as new to Bath as we are. If we don't help her, who will?"

"Mr. Page? Her nephew? That loud, emotional neighbor?" Aunt Parker rose and took Georgette's hand. "This is not your responsibility, Georgette, and we must think of our safety as well."

"Aunt Parker," Marian inserted, "if we all work together, there's no reason for any of us to be in danger. If we stand as a family, we can do what is right."

Charles cleared his throat, then told Mrs. Parker, "There is nothing I want more than to escape Bath with Georgette in tow."

"And yet," Marian said, her gaze fixed on Joseph, "leaving behind someone who needs our help isn't who we are."

Joseph groaned but finally asked the question

hanging over them. "Summarize for me *why* you think this is murder?"

Georgette told Joseph the tale of Edna Williams, her cousin, Betty, and her fears about her nephew, Kaspar.

"Do you think that this Kaspar murdered his aunt?" Joseph asked Georgette and Charles.

"He seemed very, very shocked today and distressed when he heard of Edna's theories about his Aunt Betty."

Georgette leaned over to pet the dogs while Charles listed whom they had met and the story behind each of them. As he did, Joseph was shaking his head.

"So this Edna was suggesting that the Mrs. Allyn leave her husband and take her children to *Australia?*"

Marian glanced sharply at Joseph and snapped, "He did have a second family."

"I'm not saying that's not true or that's not wrong, Marian," Joseph said. "Having your wife take your children across the world is a motive regardless of what you might have done to drive her to that choice." It said something that Joseph didn't immediately dismiss their concerns.

Georgette rubbed the back of her neck. "Anna Allyn was packing today with her children. She didn't say she was going to Australia, but she seemed to be going somewhere."

"So we have a nephew who possibly stands to gain. A highly emotional woman who lives next door and was being coaxed to leave her husband. The husband who may have discovered his wife was leaving him. All of them might have had something to do with this accident if it wasn't an accident."

"But why would Anna Allyn or her husband murder Betty?" Georgette asked Joseph, who shook his head.

"That's what we'll need to find out."

"More importantly," Georgette said, "someone needs to stay with Edna so she isn't finished off before she can say what happened. She was pretty confused when she was taken away, but what if she remembers something? If there is a killer, they have every reason to find her alone and finish her off."

CHAPTER 11

CHARLES AARON

The look on Joseph's face reflected the feeling in Charles's stomach. How did his quiet, kind, imaginative love end up pulling all of them into this madness? He wished he couldn't imagine it, but he could.

He could imagine Georgette discovering the table of her books, and he'd have loved to see her enjoy that moment. He could imagine that a person paying close attention and knowing the true name of the author would realize just who Georgette was. He could imagine Georgette being willing to have tea with that person. Of course, Georgette would be willing to experience the local teashop.

It was only then that he realized that there was

more to Edna's theory. She'd been observant enough that she had realized who Georgette was in mere moments. She wasn't a dullard like the bookseller had been. It lent credence to her theory regarding her cousin's murder.

There was something more to the connection between Georgette and people like Edna. He considered Georgette and thought—in the end—it was her eyes. She had this way of looking at you, seeing you, and listening to you. If you had a secret weighing on you and those eyes looking your way, he could see asking Georgette for help and sharing those burdens.

Marian and Joseph had left to talk to Edna, and Charles almost called them back and told them to bring Georgette. If anyone could get Edna to pour out all of her troubles, it would be Georgette.

"I'm going to take the dogs to the back garden," Georgette told him, glancing at Robert. She winked at both of them and then clucked to the dogs. She stepped into the hall and Charles turned to his nephew.

"I'm not sure Georgette can be trusted to not trip into another crime if left unsupervised."

Robert's laugh said he agreed. The way he looked guilty for his laugh had Charles biting back his own grin.

"I need you to go look at that house in Harper's Hollow. Is Eunice here with you or in London?"

"She's in London."

"Take her with you to see the house. If the house

is redeemable, buy it, and get the best price you can. You'll see by its state it needs an excessive amount of work."

"That doesn't sound like you," Robert told Charles.

He snorted as he replied, "Georgette says it *feels* right."

"Feels right?" Robert asked

Charles shook his head. You had to experience Georgette following her instincts to know that they shouldn't be discounted. He wrote down the address he'd taken note of while Georgette had been staring at the weeping willows. "My rooms won't work to take Georgette home, and this safe trip has turned into madness. When we're done here, Georgette and I are going to elope."

Robert's grin was wide, but he hid any other reaction. Charles was grateful for it. He knew that he was being irrational in his decisions as far as the house went. Marrying Georgette quickly, however, that was just good sense.

"If the house can be fixed without ruining me, and you buy it, your commission is to get it far enough along that we can live in it so that when we come back from our honeymoon, we'll be able to move in. Functional rooms, please."

Robert nodded, taking notes, and then looked up. "How bad is the house?"

"Is the fact that it 'feels' right to Georgette answer enough? There's a reason she had to use that term."

Robert winced, then adjusted his tie. "Joseph just

took his fiancé to sit with an attack victim and listen to that woman gossip, and he intends to leave Marian behind to protect the old woman."

Charles lifted a brow and waited.

"You're buying a house that you're too wise to buy on your own. And you've been chasing your Georgette all over England."

Charles gestured for Robert to finish.

"I'm never falling in love."

"I said that once."

This time, Robert was the one who winced and Charles was the one who laughed. "Go on then. We've got to get Marian and Georgette settled before they discover some cannibal gang."

"Cannibal gang?"

Robert's teasing laugh made Charles redden slightly, but the truth was he wouldn't put it past Georgette. "Don't tell her about the house. Not until we learn if I can afford it or if it's too far gone."

Robert nodded, rising. "I only came to bring you paperwork. Luther told me to come back quickly. I've even got his auto." Robert started to open the door but paused. "You know, if Georgette wants this house so badly, you shouldn't set aside what she can add."

"You think I should use her money to buy the house?" Charles asked, surprised.

"I think she'd rather have you use that money and get the house that 'feels' right," Robert said, using the quote gesture.

Charles snorted but he told Robert, "Well, you

have a pretty good idea of what she's earned. Her only indulgence has been used furniture, a few clothes, and tea."

"So she has far more than either of us would have?"

Charles shrugged, but yes—he suspected that Georgette had been far wiser than either Robert or Charles had been. It made no sense, really. She was utterly responsible—outside of tea—and then would throw it all away for a half-gone house.

~

GEORGETTE DOROTHY MARSH

Georgette paced the garden as she considered what she knew about Edna's acquaintances. Georgette simply didn't know Edna all that well. Did the woman have a dozen friends with reasons to kill her? She doubted it. Despite having seen mankind turn on each other since she'd published her first book, she just couldn't stop believing that most people were good. Like Mrs. Parker, who had never really liked Georgette all that much and yet had welcomed Georgette and Charles along with Joseph to her family.

The dogs were following Georgette as she circled the outskirts of the garden, making her the pied piper of small dogs. The sight of her girls following after her had Georgette smiling as she imagined them in that perfect garden in Harper's Hollow.

There was a part of her that wanted to plague Charles over buying that house.

Perhaps she should even—

"Georgette?"

She turned and found Harrison Parker. Georgette smiled at him. "Lovely day, isn't it? Despite everything, the sun continues to smile down on us."

Harrison cleared his throat. "I spoke to Robert this morning. He extended an offer to me to be published by Aaron and Luther."

"Oh that's wonderful!"

"I know it was you." His handsome face was unreadable and Georgette's head cocked.

"I asked Charles to read it after your last changes. Harrison, it's a good book."

"But you handed me my dream."

Georgette shook her head. "You *earned* your dream. I just asked Robert to look at you book. Aaron & Luther are professionals, Harrison. They wouldn't publish a book if it didn't have merit."

Harrison nodded. He hesitated before he spoke again. "I made a mess of things, didn't I?"

Georgette had *no* idea what he was talking about.

"I thought you were plain, and I could just ask you to read for me, and you did. It's only now that I realize I was blind."

Georgette shook her head. "Harrison, your book is good. I don't have anything to do with that."

"I thought you were plain. I thought—it's only since I've been paying attention that I realized you were more than—"

"Harrison!" Georgette said a little sharply.

"I love you, Georgette."

She stared at him and wondered what mad world she'd fallen into that he would say such things to her. He didn't love her. He didn't know her. He cared little for her and he was crediting her for things that she had not done. He was confusing excitement about his book with gratitude and a ready audience for his status.

"I know we could be happy."

She bit down on her bottom lip and then sweet Beatrice placed a paw on Georgette's foot as if realizing that Georgette was reeling. She reached down and lifted the little dog as though Beatrice could defend her against Harrison's feelings.

"I know I could make you happy, Georgette. We could have such a great life together. I know this is bad form with Charles just inside, but—"

"What is my favorite drink?"

He blinked. "Champagne? Lemonade. Yes, lemonade. Of course it is."

When she didn't nod, he guessed, "Ginger beer?"

She shook her head.

"Color?"

"What does that have to do with being in love?"

"Book?"

"Yours, of course."

Georgette's laugh was a little mean. She had moved past patience with him, past being grateful for his kindness, past all of that to sheer frustration that he wouldn't accept her no. "I don't think you

love, know, or want me any more than you want...
want...Anna Allyn."

"I don't know Mrs. Allyn. She's married."

Georgette barely contained her snort. Of course,
Anna Allyn was married. She was the first woman's
name that came to mind. It wasn't that he didn't
know Anna Allyn, it was that they both knew he
didn't know her. And yet, he barely knew Georgette
better. She strove for a soft tone. "You don't love or
know me, not really, Harrison. Isn't it possible that
you're only interested because I said no?"

"No!"

Georgette did not believe that denial for a
moment, but she said, "I think you're a good man,
Harrison Parker. You're kind to your aunt and your
cousin and to your cousin's plain friend. I am glad I
could help you and I wish you the best. Please
understand, however, I am going to marry *Charles
Aaron*—whom I love."

Harrison nodded, jaw clenching, and he stormed
out of the garden after stating, "I understand."

Slowly, Georgette pulled in a steady breath and
then blew it out. When she turned to go back inside
the house, she found Charles standing in the
shadows.

"Oh—" She closed her eyes as she asked, "Did you
see all of that?" She knew he had by the look on his
face. It was a mask that gave her no insight into what
he was thinking.

"Tea with too much milk and sugar."

Georgette's eyes were burning again and she

opened them to watch the mask melt into tenderness.

"Usually with an odd mix of flavorings that become addictive. I can almost taste that one with coffee."

Her watery laugh punctuated his step forward.

"Blue. Your favorite color is blue. The blue-grey of a sunny day with rain clouds in the distance. You like the sunny beautiful days, but the rainy ones give you peace. A combination of the two? It's your favorite."

Slowly she pressed her thumb against her chest where her heart lay. It was aching suddenly with the matching emotion in his gaze. Beatrice licked Georgette's chin and caught a tear that had slipped free.

"Your favorite book is *Persuasion* by Jane Austen, but *Pride & Prejudice* is a close second. You identify, I think too much, with both Anne and Charlotte. We can only be grateful that you don't have the family to keep you from me as poor Anne had, and I have the wit to never let you go. As for Charlotte...well, that's just laughable."

She pressed her face to the chest that was just in front of her as he spoke quietly against the top of her head.

"Your own book is not your favorite. If anything, you're confused by why other people like your writing."

She had to bite down on her bottom lip, and her shivers declared that she'd stepped into another land where she seemed to be beloved of someone.

"You are right."

"I know," he said, dropping a kiss on the top of her head. "I don't love you because of any of those things. I love you for your insight, your kindness, and the way you fit inside my heart. Knowing your favorite color and drink is just part of knowing you, and the least important parts at that."

CHAPTER 12

GEORGETTE DOROTHY MARSH

*E*dna looked as though she'd had a battle with death and lost. If not for the movement of her chest, Georgette would feel certain that the poor woman had already gone on to the next life.

"Oh my goodness." Georgette placed the bouquet of flowers on the table next to Edna and felt as though she hadn't done nearly enough. There had to be more to do. "Oh Edna, you look terrible."

A tear rolled from Edna's eye down her temple and into the tangled hair spread across the hospital pillow. "The constable doesn't believe me."

"But Joseph did?"

Edna nodded and another tear followed the first. "I have a broken collarbone, a broken arm, and broken ribs. The constable thinks I'm daft from falling down the stairs and am imagining someone—"

"Holding a pillow over your face?"

"How did you know?" The terrified look on Edna's face made it clear that Georgette was Edna's main suspect.

"I looked in your room," Georgette said calmly. "Every inch of it was in perfect order except the pillow next the wall. It seemed to me that even confused from a terrible dream you'd never have thrown the pillow over there. Or have left it if you had."

Edna's eyes widened in shock and she looked at Charles, who shook his head, but he didn't disagree.

"Georgette can do that," he told the woman. "She sees a detail like a pillow out of place and thinks 'This woman must have been nearly suffocated.' And usually, she's right."

Edna turned a questioning gaze back to Georgette.

"If you didn't throw the pillow, someone else must have," Georgette told her. "Who would be in your room without your permission unless they were doing wrong? And with Betty dying in her sleep? I just thought, well, what if she was suffocated and the doctor's missed it?"

"I woke to a pillow over my face and not being able to breathe," Edna said in a faint voice. "I struggled at first, but I realized what was happening and I pretended to twitch and held my breath. I taught swimming to the girls, you know. When I hated the work, I'd go for a swim, hold my breath, and sink under the water until my lungs hurt. I hated working there so much that I suppose I got rather good at it."

Georgette stared in horror. If Edna hadn't been able to catch her wits and fake her death, she'd have died for certain. It must have been so terrifying to pretend to be dead and hope that your killer was impatient.

"I was so lucky," Edna rasped. "I—never told anyone that. I never told anyone how I'd dream of oblivion at the girls school."

Georgette took Edna's hand. "You saved yourself. Do you have any idea of how lucky you are for being able to do that?"

It didn't seem that having hated your life and developed a terrible skill was all that comforting.

"I don't really like Bath, you know," Edna said. "I just missed my cousin. When Betty died and I thought she might have been murdered, I considered leaving so many times. Do you know why I didn't? I don't have anyone else. Anna and Kaspar are as good as it gets for me, and I thought either of them might have killed Betty."

"Why Anna?"

"Betty knew all of Anna's secrets. More than Anna has ever told me, but Betty said Anna wasn't as innocent as she seemed."

Georgette glanced at Charles and then asked, "What do you think that secret was?"

"I think Anna may have gotten pregnant on purpose to get her husband to marry her. She knew from the beginning that her husband didn't love her. He loves that girl he was raised next door to. He'd have married her eventually but for Anna."

Georgette closed her eye against the stupidity of women. But she wanted to take Anna aside and shake her silly. You didn't chase men who loved other women and expect them to adore you instead.

"I don't see that Mr. Allyn didn't know what he was doing," Charles told them both. "It's not like men don't know where babies come from. The men I know would have been flattered to have someone as outwardly beautiful and desirable as Anna Allyn chase after them."

Georgette was as unimpressed as Edna who muttered, "Idiots. I used to tell the girls that men were spoiled children who would never appreciate them. The best you can hope for is the least rotten of a bad batch of apples."

Georgette bit back a laugh at the consternation on Charles's face and then said, "You have no idea who tried to kill you?"

Edna shook her head.

"You have no idea who killed Betty?"

She shook her head again.

"Marian just stepped outside for a moment," Georgette told Edna. "She'll stay with you until we find out what is happening." After giving Edna's hand a reassuring squeeze, Georgette left the room, Charles following after her.

"She told you twice as much as she told me," Joseph said when they joined him and Marian. "She didn't say a word about Mrs. Allyn or why she lied to me."

"Georgette inspires confidence." Marian was biting back a grin and Joseph shook his head and shrugged as if he wasn't bothered at being outshone by a spinster from a small town.

"Georgette does have a way about her," Joseph agreed. "Which might be useful as I'm not officially on this case."

"What does that mean, 'be useful'?" Charles's hesitation was enough for Joseph to slap him on the shoulder and say, "You can come too."

"Come where?" Charles didn't seem any more relieved because they were going to be interfering as a group.

"To visit the nephew and the neighbor and provide condolences."

Charles groaned.

"Our girls don't want to leave Bath if Edna is undefended."

Marian grinned and saluted the others. "Speaking of, I believe that's my cue to return to the feisty victim."

"You have what I gave you?" Joseph's gaze was intent.

Marian patted her handbag.

"Protect her if you can, but you're my priority."

"This is a fiend with a pillow who strikes while old women sleep," Marian told Joseph. She sounded entirely fearless. "I doubt we'll be in trouble as long as she remains with someone nearby."

"Don't leave her," Georgette said. "Not for anyone."

Marian was nodding before Georgette had even finished stating the words. Joseph placed a soft kiss on Marian's lips as Charles held out his arm to Georgette. They took a black cab back to Edna's house, but they walked up the steps to Anna Allyn's house instead.

"Do you think she killed Betty and tried to kill Edna?" Joseph asked in a whisper.

Georgette looked at Joseph and then shook her head.

Anna answered after the second round of knocking. "Can I help you?" Her face was sweaty, her cheeks flushed, and her hair was wrapped in a kerchief.

"We visited Edna in the hospital and thought you might like to hear how she is."

Anna looked over her shoulder, and Georgette could hear the sound of a little boy crying. Slowly, Anna opened the door and Georgette saw the child sitting on the stairs, clutching a teddy bear, eyes swollen as though he'd been sobbing for the entirety of the day.

"Ignore Hal," Anna said. "He's still adjusting to the idea of an adventure in Australia."

"I don't want to leave my daddy!" the boy shouted. "I don't want to go!"

"Your daddy shouldn't have another family,"

Anna shouted back. "He doesn't care about you or me or Lee! He only cares about that whore and the other children."

"I hate you!" Hal shouted. "I hate you, I hate you, I hate you."

Anna turned to Georgette, Joseph, and Charles who were all looking on in shock and snapped, "What? He'll get over it."

Georgette hardly thought so, but she closed her eyes and breathed in deeply to steady herself. "Did you try to kill Edna? Did you kill Betty?"

"What? Why would I?"

"Betty knew that you tried to trick Mr. Allyn into marriage."

"Betty *thought* I tried to trick Dennis into marriage. She saw me as an idiot. Some...some... cow who gave the milk too soon. That wasn't what happened. I wouldn't have killed Betty for believing that and Edna lent me the money I needed to leave."

"I hate her!" Hal screamed. "I hate her and I hate you."

"This isn't a good time," Anna snapped. "What do you want from me? Do you need to know I'm stupid? You know that already. Everyone in Bath who knows me knows that about me! Do you need to know that Dennis wouldn't have done anything to Edna or Betty? Because he wants us to go. He wants me to divorce him. He wants to marry that whore and start over in Kent. 'Take the children, Anna,'" she mimicked. "'I'll send you money.' That was a lie of course. The only reason we can go is because I took the money from our joint account, sold the jewelry he gave me and everything we had of value. He isn't going to send me a cent or ever help with Hal and Lee."

Georgette winced. "What are you going to do in Australia?"

Anna sighed in resignation. "Marry another man who doesn't love me and hope he'll be kinder than Dennis and love my children even though they aren't his."

Georgette held herself back from shaking Anna silly, but only just.

"What about Kaspar?" Georgette asked. Anna's eyes widened, and Georgette realized what that had sounded like. "Do you think he might have killed Betty and tried to kill Edna?" she clarified. She couldn't let herself be distracted with the idea of Kaspar marrying Anna.

Anna looked at her sobbing child, glanced through the open door to the parlor where her other child looked as though he'd cried himself to sleep and said quietly, "I don't really care. I don't have it in me right now. Edna is alive. I mourned Betty a while ago, and every other part of my life has fallen apart. I suppose I'm too selfish to do anything more than send her my good thoughts and keep myself and my children from falling entirely to pieces."

"Good luck," Georgette said, but she didn't leave. She crossed to Hal, squatted down, and whispered, "None of this is your fault. Both of your parents love you."

He stared at her with wide watery eyes, and she knew there was nothing that she could say that would make this moment less devastating, so she kissed him on the forehead. "It'll get better. I promise, it'll get better someday."

She left Anna's house without looking back, because if Georgette dared to eye the soon-to-be divorcée, she might just wring the woman's neck for causing that broken look in her son's eyes. Rather than get back in the black cab, she called, "I need a moment."

She crossed the street to a minuscule little green space with a stone bench and sat down, pressing her face into her hands. She wasn't crying, but she was shaking. There was so much hurt in not being loved. In being the extraneous woman who was left to fend for herself. Georgette had realized long ago that the fate of some married women was worse. She didn't like to think too much about it, but she had known it was true.

"Are you all right, my dear?"

Georgette looked up and found Mr. Page.

"It's just hard."

"The fate of an unmarried woman is very difficult. You have to fend for yourself. I understand you turned down Mr. Parker's offer of marriage. You should be aware that he was doing you quite an honor, my dear."

Georgette felt as though she'd been transported to some version of Hades as she looked up at Mr. Page.

"Don't you think that loving each other matters?"

"Love comes with time."

"It didn't for Anna and Dennis Allyn."

Mr. Page gave Georgette a derisive look. "Mrs. Allyn needs to content herself with her home, her children, and her husband."

"Her husband is stepping out on her," Georgette shot back. "He's having children with another woman and neglecting those he has with Anna."

"Would he if she were attending to her duties? I can assure you that I have known Anna Allyn since she married her husband and joined us here. She has complained from the beginning."

Attending to her duties? Georgette swallowed back a curse, realizing that Mr. Page was a man of the old-school and there would be no changing his outlook by some pithy remark any more than there would be for comforting little Hal Allyn.

She stood. "Good day, Mr. Page."

CHAPTER 13

GEORGETTE DOROTHY MARSH

"*I*'m not quite sure how to get Kaspar Williams to answer our questions," Joseph said as Georgette returned to them.

"Let's go back to Mrs. Parker's home and have lunch. Maybe we'll be struck by inspiration. At the very least," Charles told them, "we'll need to contact Edna or Mr. Page and discover where Kaspar is staying."

Georgette shuddered at the thought of speaking again to Mr. Page, but she said nothing. Lunch was a quiet affair, and Georgette took the afternoon to go up to her shared room and start her new book. Charles and Joseph had decided to visit the local constables in the guise of seeing if there was merit to their *fiancées'* concerns and see what they could ferret out. They intended to drop a note by Kaspar's hotel and invite him to come by that evening for drinks. Hopefully they'd be able to pin him down and persuade somewhat reasonable answers out of him.

Georgette worked until Marian knocked on the bedroom door. "We'll be having dinner soon."

Georgette twisted to stare at Marian. "Did you leave Edna alone?"

"I told the nurses our concerns and how the local constables didn't believe us. Dismissed us as silly women. That was all it took. They arranged a series of nurses to stay with Edna until she was released from the hospital. Her bed was moved, so there will be no sneaking up on Edna without someone seeing, and they were cosseting her when I left." Marian gave her a smile and left the room.

Georgette relaxed, but only a little. The start of Georgette's new story had turned distinctly sour and sad with a boy rather like Hal losing his parents and contracting a terrible illness. Georgette stared at the pages and then tossed them into the rubbish bin before changing her dress, brushing her hair, and following Marian down the stairs.

Dinner was quiet. Harrison and Mrs. Parker had decided to visit one of the local restaurants that had a celebrated French chef, but Georgette had little doubt that Harrison was avoiding her. They had been joined by Mr. Page who seemed a bit at loose ends with Edna in the hospital or had simply wished more time with Mrs. Parker.

Georgette felt bad about driving poor Harrison off. She was the interloper in this house, not Harrison, but her presence was sending him away.

Joseph spoke as they ate. "I understand you love Harper's Hollow. I did as well."

Charles glanced at Georgette and she noticed something in his gaze. She looked a question, but he just smiled at her.

"Charles is going to buy a rowboat," Marian said significantly.

"Perfect," Joseph said, leaning back with his wine glass, "then we won't have to."

Marian knew Joseph was teasing her, so she ignored it.

"We could buy a house, however. I contacted a man and told him our budget and what we were looking for."

Her eyes widened.

"First, however, we need to leave here. Bath doesn't seem as healthy as it is purported to be."

They finished their dinner and took refuge in the parlor with more wine, cigarettes for Marian and Joseph, a pipe for Charles, and a pen and paper for Georgette. She sketched out ideas for her next book, but she couldn't help but find herself writing a story about another spinster.

What if she did, she thought as she wrote out a list of names to see if they sparked a character in Georgette's head. *Clara. Sarah.* No. Not those. *Otto-*

line. The half-German daughter of a...of an... accountant. Her mother had died when she was quite small. No. Not that one.

Georgette's mouth twisted as she wrote out more names: *Hester. Violet. Fallow. Mina.* No, Georgette thought, *Wilhelmina Francesca.* One of many children. Perhaps the seventh daughter, but not the last daughter. Perhaps...lost in her family?

Lost in her family and a spinster? No. *Hero.* Daughter of a literary professor who adored Shakespeare. *Maud. Lily. Alma. Ernestine. Nora. Mavis.* Georgette's mouth twisted again. Ideas were sparking, but she rejected them almost immediately.

"What's this?"

Georgette glanced up and found Charles reading over her shoulder. He was followed by Marian.

"Are these baby names?"

"Ottoline?" Charles sounded horrified.

"Character names," Georgette laughed. "Josephine wasn't intended to be a series and I think it's time to retire Bard's Crook."

"What if you didn't?" Charles asked. "At least until our house is settled."

Georgette paused and then her head tilted. "Were you thinking of an expensive house? Perhaps one that needs some work?"

Joseph laughed, which gave Charles away, but he kept his expression smooth as he answered. "Regardless of where we buy and what is possible, another Bard's Crook just might buy furniture."

"I do enjoy writing in Bard's Crook."

She also enjoyed the idea of buying a pair of olive leather chesterfields for their parlor. Perhaps a really nice iron bed for their room. Something made by artisans with branches or whatnot. What about if when she got stuck on her Bard's Crook stories, she wrote a story about—

"Vega," Georgette said aloud. "Or Tiggy?"

"Tiggy." Marian grinned. "I love it and her already. I want the stories of Tiggy. I want to read her adventures."

Georgette laughed and gave Charles a sly look. "Perhaps a dash of Bard's Crook with a side of Tiggy will get a new roof. Or paper in the library. That ladder looked askew, but surely a handy sort of fellow can step in and fix it."

"Nothing is certain," Charles started to tell her, but there was a knock at the door and Joseph rose to answer it. He led Kaspar into the parlor, immediately lighting him a cigarette and handing it over.

"The nurses wouldn't let me see Edna this evening," Kaspar said with a sigh. "I told her that I would never hurt her, but—"

He seemed quite upset, but as much as Georgette wanted to believe his upset, perhaps he was simply a good actor. "Well, you argued with Betty before she died—"

"Not about something you *kill* over," Kaspar huffed. "Betty didn't approve of my girl. We argued. I told Betty I loved Daisy and I was going to marry her, and Betty told me I would regret it as much as Dennis Allyn regretted marrying Anna."

126

"So what happened?"

"I stormed out. I went to ask Daisy to marry me. I was going to bring her back to Betty and...and... make Betty love her."

"And?"

"Daisy was out. She was a typist, and I heard she might be at the teashop having a cuppa and a bun, so I followed her."

Georgette had little doubt, given the sour twist to his mouth, that the story didn't end well.

"What happened?" Marian asked softly.

Charles and Joseph seemed to sense the answer because Joseph handed Kaspar a fresh cigarette and Charles pushed a tumbler of whiskey into his hand.

Kaspar hung his head. "She was kissing her boss in the alcove next to the teashop. He was married, of course. She ended up in trouble, and Betty ended up saving me."

Georgette wondered how they could confirm that story, but Kaspar seemed to have already thought that problem out because he said, "You know, Edna didn't know it, but Betty changed her will to favor Edna over me."

"Did she?" Georgette asked gently. "Were you upset?"

"No," Kaspar scoffed. "I have a good position. I don't need the few pence Betty had beyond the house."

"Can anyone confirm that story?" Joseph asked. He took a deep puff on his cigarette, which removed any intensity from the question.

"The solicitor," Kaspar muttered. "I told Betty to invite Edna when Betty mentioned how lonely she was. When my father died, he asked me to look after them. A widow and a spinster. No male friends. How he must be looking down on me in disgust. Betty dead, Edna in the hospital afraid of me. A deathbed promise that I can't keep."

Kaspar took a large gulp of the whiskey and then coughed as though it burned a little too much. Georgette sighed as she studied him. His story was utterly verifiable, and it explained why he bothered with Edna, who really didn't enjoy his presence.

"What do you think about Anna Allyn and her husband? Would Dennis Allyn have tried to keep Edna from assisting his wife back to Australia?"

Kaspar scoffed again. "He's been trying to drive Anna home to her family for at least a year or two. If he realized that Edna was going to hand over whatever she has squirreled away to help Anna leave, he'd probably drop to his knees in utter joy."

"Fabulous," Georgette muttered under her breath. She had very much wanted to trap Kaspar and have him arrested for murdering Betty and hurting Edna. That way she and Charles could escape into the dawn to be wed without delay. Perhaps even, she thought, into that house that had felt so right.

Joseph stepped in and questioned Kaspar from every possible side, but there was nothing to say. He'd stopped by Edna's home to tell her he was leaving. He found her moaning and bruised on the stairs and stumbled outside the house.

Georgette had already moved beyond Kaspar, but with the information they had already about the Allyns, there was nowhere left to go. They didn't know enough about Edna in order to answer questions about her life or find those who might have had a motive to murder her. She'd spoken of a few others during their tea and then only in passing like they were barely acquaintances. There was, of course, Mr. Page, but what reason would he have? It is true he seemed attached to Edna at first, but he was spending more time with Aunt Parker. She'd seen no reason for him to wish Edna dead, and he'd barely spoken a word about Betty. As it was, he had been on a walk with Edna when Betty died.

What if, however, the real target was Betty and Edna figured out what happened to her? But no, Georgette thought, no. Edna would have said so at the hospital, wouldn't she? It was true that Edna hadn't been as forthcoming in the beginning as Georgette would have hoped, but since admitting her fears about her cousin's death, she had been open without a hint of deception.

"None of this makes sense," Kaspar muttered. "Why hurt a couple of useless old ladies who only matter to a few?"

Georgette gasped and then bit down on her lip to prevent another tirade. Charles sent a dark look at Joseph, who got rid of Kaspar moments later.

"Octavia," Georgette announced once Kaspar was gone. "The spinster who matters to a few. She'll be like Edna who helps others."

Georgette rose and glanced back at Charles. "I'll bring her into Bard's Crook and then move her to a new village. What do you think?"

"I like it. Will you give her a baffled lover?"

She didn't answer, but she didn't answer on purpose. As the evening finished, Joseph and Charles left—entirely unbothered that Georgette got sucked into her story. Marian went to bed. Harrison and Aunt Parker came back and went to bed without even noticing Georgette scribbling away with a pen and paper, wishing for her typewriter.

CHAPTER 14

GEORGETTE DOROTHY MARSH

"Motive," Georgette muttered. She'd been sketching out ideas for Octavia's backstory and had stood up to pace. What did Octavia do? Was she a childless widow like Betty? Was she a school teacher like Edna? Did she have a bit of family money? Who did these days? Perhaps Georgette should set her story earlier. What about a Victorian woman who...who...solved mysteries rather like Joseph?

Her lips thinned into a line. Motive, Georgette thought. That was the problem with all of this as far as Edna and Betty went. When someone murdered a person who was young and beautiful like Anna Allyn, you assumed she'd have a romance. When someone murdered an older man, you assumed he'd been dishonorable.

Georgette frowned as she paced, losing track of Octavia for Edna and Betty. Why had Edna survived? She'd lived because she held her breath and faked death. And why could she do that? Because she despised her life as much as any young, pretty Anna Allyn might.

"What if Betty had a lover?" she asked the empty room. The fact that Georgette hesitated to believe that Betty might have been in love had her scolding herself. You could fall in love at any age.

Georgette immediately thought of Mr. Page. He was an odd man. Really, he was also the last one left. The last of the possible killers. Edna had so few friends. Mr. Page lived just there on the same street. He'd been offended that Georgette had turned down Harrison Parker.

What if, Georgette wondered, Mr. Page had asked Betty to marry him? What if Betty turned him down, sidestepped the love he proffered, and not been grateful? It was mad to think of a man murdering a woman for turning down his marriage offer. And yet—women were most often hurt not by strangers but by those who pretended to love them.

He'd seemed close to Edna during the tea, Georgette recalled. But then what about Mrs. Parker? Mr. Page seemed to be pursuing her, not Edna. Georgette was ashamed that she'd assumed they were only looking for card partners, but if she'd witnessed the same pursuit for someone young and lovely like

Marian, the man inviting himself to dinners, stopping by unannounced, Georgette wouldn't have just thought, 'oh, he's interested in her.' She'd have thought he was a little uncomfortably interested in her.

Without thinking about the lateness of the hour, Georgette hurried up the steps to Aunt Parker's room, careful not to trip in the dark. She tapped on the door lightly so that if Aunt Parker wasn't awake, she wouldn't be disturbed. Instead Georgette heard, "Come in."

Georgette sidestepped into the room. Aunt Parker was wearing an old plaid nightgown with a white collar and a kerchief over her hair but was sitting in a chair in the room, the bed still neat.

"I have the oddest question," Georgette said.

"Distract me," Aunt Parker said. "I am quite encompassed in my thoughts, my dear."

Georgette pressed her lips together before asking, "Would that be because of Mr. Page's pursuit?"

Aunt Parker blushed furiously. "How did you know?"

Georgette didn't want to offend Aunt Parker, but the worry was rising. The fact of the matter was, Georgette thought, there were really only a few likely suspects for who might have killed Betty and hurt Edna and they'd ruled out all of the obvious ones. Only Mr. Page was left.

"Why?" Aunt Parker demanded again with more than a little concern. "How did you know?"

"I was thinking of him and how he might be pursuing you. I wondered if he pursued Betty and Edna the same." She expected Aunt Parker to throw her out for being so blunt, but she only gave a great sigh.

"He asked me to marry him," Aunt Parker admitted. "No, not asked. He said it rather like Marian describes how Harrison asked you to marry him. He started planning our life together without any reference to what I wanted. I mean, I *just* met the man, and I'm supposed to leave my plans to live near my daughter and join him here? We'd take a week every year on the Mediterranean Sea, he said. I would move into his house and wouldn't need any of my own things. I would be happier with him instead of living alone. He just…just assumed."

"Did you say no?"

Aunt Parker laughed. "I understood you immediately, my dear. I told Harrison you deserved to be adored like all women do. He told me he tried again."

"I didn't tell him no specifically because he assumed I would be grateful. I told him no because I am marrying Charles, whom I love."

Aunt Parker nodded. "My own husband died years ago, but I remember being loved and loving. A pale imitation is of no interest to me."

Georgette didn't disagree. She sagged somewhat in relief that Aunt Parker hadn't given in so easily, but her mind was already piecing together her suspicions with facts.

"May I get you some hot milk or something to

help you sleep?" she asked Aunt Parker distractedly. She was thinking of how to contact Joseph and Charles this late at night. "Chamomile tea with warm milk? Sort of half and half mix?"

"That does sound nice," Aunt Parker agreed.

Georgette went down to the kitchen to make tea and warm milk. She didn't have the telephone number of where Charles and Joseph were staying, an oversight she wouldn't make again. Charles would be irate if she dared to put herself at risk by walking to his hotel so late at night.

Surely she could wait until morning. She'd take tea up to Aunt Parker's room and they'd sit and chat until Aunt Parker was too tired to continue. Georgette, however, was determined to stay awake, so when she made tea, she made the chamomile for Aunt Parker and a good, strong English Breakfast tea for herself.

She poured them both a healthy mug and moved back up the stairs. She stopped short at the top.

Tea.

Mr. Page had shared tea with Edna and Betty just before Betty died. He'd been out for a walk with Edna, an easy alibi. And Betty was older and had been ill. No one would think to check for poison.

Georgette went cold, then hurried onward. As she passed the room she shared with Marian, she heard the dogs whining. She didn't want them to wake Marian and they'd be welcome company as she kept watch over Aunt Parker in case Mr. Page were to try something. She rather doubted it. It would be too obvious at this point, but she wouldn't take the chance.

She set Aunt Parker's mug on the narrow table in the hall and opened the door to let the dogs out. They darted around her to Aunt Parker's door. Georgette froze in terror. They had never done that before.

Surely this wasn't happening. Not now, when she had just come to understand the truth. Steeling herself, Georgette pushed open the bedroom door. Dorcas and Beatrice darted in, chased by Marian's dog and Susan. Georgette followed to find all four dogs growling and barking at Mr. Page, who stood over Aunt Parker sprawled on the bed with a pillow held over her face.

"Mr. Page!" Georgette shouted.

He did not remove his hand. Aunt Parker's struggles were weakening. Georgette did the first things that came to mind. She screamed for Harrison and threw the tea at Mr. Page.

Mr. Page stumbled away as the hot tea scalded him. "She deserves it!" Mr. Page shouted with insane fury.

Georgette didn't answer as she darted to Aunt Parker, grabbed her hand, and hauled her off the bed and into her arms. Aunt Parker was so weak that she sagged to the floor.

"You deserve it," Georgette told him coldly. She'd have dropped to her knees to check on Aunt Parker, but the man was too close and too dangerous. Aunt Parker was breathing and crying, but she was alive.

"Who do you think you are? A woman doesn't love you, so you murder her?"

Georgette's words were punctuated by Marian's gasp in the doorway. She was shoved aside as Harrison darted into the room in a striped night-gown. He took one look at them and then roughly grabbed hold of Mr. Page and shook him until the old man's teeth rattled.

"Call for the constables," Georgette told Marian, who went running. Georgette didn't bother to ask for Charles. She had little doubt that Marian would call for Joseph as well and Charles would appear. Georgette dropped to her knees and wrapped her arms around Aunt Parker. "It's all right, darling. Everything will be all right."

The frenzy of the evening passed with constables taking away Mr. Page. Marian chased them to the street, scolding them the entire way for setting aside Edna's fears and her attack. Georgette had little doubt that the constables would not make the same mistake.

By the time Mr. Page had been escorted away without a fight, Joseph and Charles had arrived. Aunt Parker was sitting between Georgette and Harrison, clutching each of them by the hand while the doctor looked her over.

"You'll be all right, Mrs. Parker," the doctor said after a while, prescribing her sleeping medicine.

"I am ready to leave Bath," Georgette told Charles. He nodded as though he would pack her clothes himself.

"As am I," Aunt Parker said, her voice weak. "I'll stay with my daughter if I must."

"I do need to get back to work," Harrison admitted. There was a flash of an excited grin that he quickly shoved away as he glanced at his aunt. "I'm not a dog person, Aunt, but you're getting a big, protective one."

She seemed entranced with the idea. "A dog. And a ready cup of hot tea. Possibly with surprisingly fierce nieces nearby."

"This one," Charles told Aunt Parker with a fond look to Georgette, "is going to go home with me."

Aunt Parker smiled at him. "I understand entirely."

CHARLES HAD OBTAINED the marriage license when Georgette had agreed to marry him, so all they had to do was pack their things, take an auto, and drive back to London. They were married in a small church with only a few guests, though a few more than they'd planned. Aunt Parker refused to miss the event.

Georgette's simple dress combined with her happiness left her stunning. The glow of her eyes, her usually hidden smile at the forefront, and the bouquet of pure white roses all added to the effect of her joy.

Which she didn't think could be greater until Charles handed her the deed to her Harper's Hollow house. Her mouth dropped open and Charles laughed as he pressed a kiss to the top of her head.

"The price was right," he told her.

"It felt right, too," she told him, guessing that there was more than a low sale price to convince him.

"That too." The smile he gave her was full of love. "I'm wise enough to look back at my life before you came into it and see that while it had been easier and it had been smoother, it had been far less filled with joy. But you—" He paused to kiss her, then pressed his forehead against hers. "You give me joy, love, brightness, excitement to face the day. I am determined to do the same for you. Surely the first and easiest step is to give you the house you treasure."

With tears in her eyes, Georgette laid her head against his chest. She had never felt so loved and cherished. She knew in her heart that together—if they were determined—surely a happily ever after was not just possible, not just achievable, but a certainty.

So often, those who had followed the normal path of early marriage and children assumed that the long-time singles would be too unbending in binding lives together. How wrong they were—those unimaginative souls. If they took a moment of self-examination, they'd know that they looked at the Georgettes of the world and thought, how nice it would be to not have to deal with my husband's bad habits. How nice it would be to not have children screaming and dirtying up what I just cleaned.

The Georgettes of the world knew, however, what the heart felt like before children and after. They recognized the joy of being a mother after having spent so long watching others become mothers instead. They knew the comfort of having someone to turn to and discuss the woes of life, the decisions of life, the simple day-to-day moments.

Mankind was not meant to be alone, but it was rare for anyone who hadn't been alone to recognize how nice it was simply to join another in a parlor, work in unison, and then lift up the head, turn to their love, and offer a cup of tea.

Atë blinked away tears as her favorite wed. As a goddess, she'd been able to tell that Georgette would most likely choose Charles. As a goddess, she could see the paths that rolled out before them. In the realm of possibilities, there were outside chances for bad ends. The probabilities, however, favored happiness. Especially as each of them determined to put the other first, love the other fiercely, and always remember what it had been like to be alone.

The END

AUTHOR'S NOTE

*H*ullo, my friends, I have so much gratitude for you reading my books. Almost as wonderful as giving me a chance are reviews, and indie folks, like myself, need them desperately! If you wouldn't mind, I would be so grateful for a review.

THE SEQUEL to this book is available now. Or, if you want book updates, you could follow me on Facebook.

July 1937

Georgette Dorothy Parker has found her dream home, her dream village, and her dream husband. She and Charles purchase their house, move, and the discover all isn't as it seems.

Have they found *another* village with dark secrets? Is their happily ever after going to fade so soon? Will they be able to uncover what is happening or have they made a terrible mistake?

Order Here.

IF YOU ENJOY mysteries with a historical twist, scroll to the end for a sample of my new mystery series, The Hettie and Ro Adventures. The first book, Philanderers Gone is now available.

July 1922

If there's one thing to draw you together, it's shared misery.

Hettie and Ro married manipulative, lying, money-grubbing pigs. Therefore, they were instant friends. When those philandering dirtbags died, they found themselves the subjects of a murder investigation. Did they kill their husbands? No. Did they joke about it? Maybe. Do they need to find the killer before the crime is pinned on them? They do!

Join Hettie and Ro and their growing friendship as they delve into their own lives to find a killer, a best friend, and perhaps a brighter new outlook.

Order Here.

PHILANDERERS GONE
PREVIEW

The house was one of those ancient stone artisan-crafted monstrosities that silently, if garishly, announced buckets of bullion, ready money, the green, call it what you would, these folks were simply rolling in the good life. The windows were stained glass with roses and stars. The floor of wide-planked dark wood was probably Egyptian wood carried by camels and horses through deserts to the house. The furnishings were as finely dressed as the people gathered in celebration.

Hettie hid a smirk when a tall, beautiful, uniformed man slid through the crowd and leaned down, holding a tray of champagne and cocktails in front of her with a lascivious gaze. She wasn't quite sure if he appreciated the irony of his status as human art for the party, or if he embraced it and the opportunity it gave him to romance bored wives.

She was, very much, a bored wife. Or maybe disillusioned was the proper word. She took yet another flute of champagne and curled into the chair, pulling up her legs, leaving her shoes behind, and tucking her feet under her.

The sight of her husband laughing uproariously with a drink in each hand made her want to skip over to him and toss her champagne into his face. He had been drinking and partying so heavily, he'd become yellowed. The dark circles under his eyes emphasized his utter depravity. Or, then again, perhaps that was the disillusionment once again. Which came first? The depravity or the dark circles?

"Fiendish brute," Hettie muttered, lifting her glass at her own personal animal. Her husband, Harvey, wrapped his arm around another bloke, laughing into his face so raucously the poor man must have felt as though he'd stepped into a summer rain storm reeking of booze.

"Indeed," a woman said, and Hettie flinched, biting back a gasp to twist and see who had over-heard her.

What a shocker! If Hettie had realized that anyone was around instead of swimming in that drunken sea of flesh, she'd have insulted him non-verbally. It was quite satisfying to speak her feelings out loud. Heaven knew he deserved every ounce of criticism.

She had nothing against fun. She had nothing

against dancing, jazz, cocktails, or adventure. She did, however, have quite a lot against Harvey.

He had discovered her in Quebec City. Or rather he'd discovered she was an heiress and then pretended to discover her. He'd written her love letters and poems praising her green eyes, her red hair, and her pale skin as though being nearly dead-girl white were something to be envied. He'd made her feel beautiful even though she tended towards the plump, and he'd seemed oblivious to the spots she'd been dealing with on her chin and jaw line through all of those months.

A fraud in more ways than Hettie could count, he'd spent months prostrating himself at her feet, romancing her, wearing down her defenses until she'd strapped on the old white dress and discovered she'd gotten a drunken, spoiled, rude, lying ball and chain.

"Do you hate him too?" Hettie asked, wondering if she were commiserating with one of her husband's lovers. She would hardly be surprised.

"Oh, so much," the woman said. Her gaze met Hettie's and then they snorted almost in unison. "Such a wart. Makes everything a misery. It's a wonder that someone has not clocked him over the back of the head yet."

Hettie shocked herself with a laugh, totally unprepared to adore one of her husband's mistresses. "Oh! If only!" She lifted her glass in toast to the woman who grinned and lifted her own in return. "Cheers, darling."

"So, are you one of his lovers?" the woman asked.

"Wife," Hettie said, and the woman's gaze widened.

"Wife? I hardly think so."

"Oh, believe me," Hettie replied. "I wish it wasn't so."

"As his wife," the woman said with a frown, "I fear I must dispute your claim."

Hettie's gaze narrowed and she glanced back at Harvey. His blonde hair had been pomaded back, but some hijinks had caused the seal on the pomade to shift and it was flopping about in greasy hanks. He and the man he'd been molesting earlier clinked their glasses together and guzzled the cocktails. Harvey leaned into the man, and they both laughed raucously.

"Idiot," the woman said scornfully. "Look at him gulping down a drink that anyone with taste would have sipped. The blonde one, he must be yours?"

Hettie nodded with disgust and grimaced. "Unfortunately, yes, the blond wart with the pomade gone wrong is my ball and chain. So the other fool is yours?"

The woman laughed. "I suppose I sounded almost jealous. I wasn't, you know. I'd have been happy if Leonard was yours."

"Alas, my fate has been saddled with yon blond horse, Harvey."

They grinned at each other and then the other woman held out her hand. "Ro Lavender. So pleased to meet someone with my same ill-fate. Makes me feel less alone."

Hettie held out her own hand. "Hettie Hughes. I thought Leonard's last name was Ripley."

"Oh, it is," Ro said. "I try not to tie myself to his wagon unless it benefits me. At the bank, for instance."

"Shall we be bosom friends?" Hettie asked.

"I just read that book. Do you love it as well?"

"I'm Canadian," Hettie replied, standing to twine her arm through Ro's. "Of course I've read it. Anne, Green Gables, Diana, Gilbert, Marilla, and Prince Edward Island were fed to me with milk as a babe. Only those of us with a fiendish brute for a husband can truly understand the agony of another. How did you get caught?"

"Family pressure. We were raised together. Quite close friends over the holidays, but I never knew the real him until after."

Hettie winced. "Love letters for me," she said disgustedly. "You'd think modern women such as ourselves wouldn't have been quite so…"

"Stupid," Ro replied, tucking her bobbed hair behind her ear.

The laughter from the crowd around the table became too much to hear anything and Hettie asked, "Shall we escape into the nighttime?"

"Let's go to Prince Edward Island," Ro joked. "Is it magical there? I've always wanted to go."

"I've never been," Hettie admitted, "but I have a sudden desperate need. Let's flee in the darkness.

You know they won't miss us until their fathers insist they arrive somewhere with their respectable wives on their arms."

"Or, I could murder yours and you could murder mine, and we could create our freedom. If our families want respectable, I would definitely respect a woman that could rid herself of these monsters."

"That sounds lovely. Until we can plan our permanent freedom, I suppose our best option is simply to retreat."

Ro lifted her glass in salute and sipped.

Hettie set aside her champagne flute and then turned to face her husband, who had pulled Mrs. Stone, the obvious trollop, into his lap and was kissing her extravagantly. Hettie scrunched up her nose and gagged a little. Mrs. Stone had been in Nathan Brighton's lap just last week.

"She slept with Leonard too," Ro informed Hettie in an even tone.

Hettie reveled in the camaraderie she found in Ro's resigned tone. "Have you met Mr. Stone?"

Ro nodded. "He doesn't realize. He's not the type of man to be cuckolded like this. So…overtly. Have you heard of the marriage act they've proposed?"

Hettie nodded with little doubt that her eyes had brightened like that of a child at Christmas. "I will be there on the very first day. If Harvey had any idea, any at all, he'd be rolling over in his future grave. The money's mine, you know? My aunt never liked Harvey and she tied up my money tightly. He gets what he wants because it's easier to give it to him than listen to him whine, but he won't get a half-penny from me the day I can file divorce papers. They say it's going to go through."

"I couldn't care less about the money," Ro replied. "Though my money is coming from a still-living aunt. Leonard has enough, I suppose, but his eye is definitely on Aunt Bette's fortune."

"So he needs to go before she does."

Ro choked on her laughter so hard she had to wipe away tears.

"Darling!" Harvey hollered across the room. "We're going down to Leonard's yacht. You can get yourself home, can't you?"

Hettie closed her eyes for a moment before she replied. "Of course I can. Don't fall in." She crossed her fingers so only Ro could see. Ro's laugh made Hettie grin at Harvey. He gave her a bit of a confused look. Certainly he had shouted his exit with the hope she wouldn't scold him. Foolish man! She'd welcome him moving into Mrs. Stone's bed permanently and leaving Hettie behind.

The handsome servant from earlier picked up Hettie's abandoned glass and shot her a telling, not quite disapproving look.

"Oh-ho," Hettie said, making sure the man heard her. "We've been overheard."

"We've been eavesdropped," Ro agreed. Then with a lifted brow to the human work of art serving champagne, "Boyo, our husbands are aware of our lack of love. There's no chance for blackmail here."

"Does your aunt feel the same?" he asked insinu-atingly.

Hettie stiffened, but Ro only laughed. "Do you think she hasn't heard the tale of that lush Leonard? She's written me stiff-upper-lip letters. 'Watch your step and your mouth or you'll lose your position despite your pretty face,'" she repeated in a pinched tone. "'It doesn't matter how you feel, only how you look. No one is paying you to think.'"

The servant flushed and bowed deeply, shooting them both a furious expression as he silently backed away.

"Cheeky lad," Hettie muttered. "You scolded him furiously. Are you sure you weren't taking out your rage on the poor fellow?"

"Cheeky, yes," Ro agreed. She placed a finger on her lip as she considered Hettie's question and then agreed. "Too harsh as well. I suppose I would need to apologize if he didn't threaten to blackmail me."

"But pretty," they said nearly in unison. They laughed as the servant overhead them and gave them both a sultry glance.

"Oh no, boyo," Ro told him. "Toddle off now, darling. We've had quite our fill of philandering, reckless men. You've missed your window." Ro's head cocked as she glanced Hettie over. "Well, shall we?"

"Shall we what, love?"

Ro grinned wickedly. "Shall we be bosom friends? Soul sisters after one shared breath?"

"Let's. As the man I thought was my soulmate

was an utter disaster, I'll take a soul sister as a replacement."

They sent a servant to get an auto. "I was thinking of going to a bottle party later," Ro told her. "At a bath house. That just might distract us."

Hettie tilted her head as she considered. "Harvey does expect me to go home."

Ro lifted her brows and waited.

"So we must, of course, disillusion him as perfectly as he has me."

"There we go!" Ro cheered, shaking her hands over head. "It is only fair. I have been considering a trip to the Paris fashion salons."

"Yes," Hettie immediately agreed, knowing it would enrage Harvey, who preferred her tucked away in case he needed her. "We should linger in Paris then swing over to Spain."

"Oooh, Spain!"

"Italy," Hettie suggested just to see if Ro would agree.

"Yes!"

"Russia?"

Ro paused. "Perhaps Cote d'Azure? Egypt? Somewhere warmer. I always think of snow when I think of Russia, and I only like it with cocoa and sleigh rides. Perhaps one or two days a year."

"Agreed—" Hettie trailed off, eyes wide, as she watched Mrs. Stone enthusiastically kiss the cheeky servant from earlier and then adjust her coat. She winked at Hettie on the way out, caring little that both of them knew Mrs. Stone would be climbing into Harvey's bed later. Or perhaps it was Harvey who would be climbing into Mr. Stone's bed. "Is her husband really blind to it?"

"Oh yes." Ro laughed. "He's quite a bit older, you know, and even more old-fashioned than my grandfather. He's Victorian through and through. He probably has a codicil in the will about her remarrying. The type of thing that cuts her off if she doesn't remain true to him. Especially since he's in his seventies, and she's thirty? Perhaps?"

Hettie shook her head and put Mrs. Stone from her mind. "They have a rather outstanding blackberry wine here. Shall we just—ah—borrow a bottle or two for the party?"

Ro nodded and walked across to the bar, digging through the bottles to pull out a full bottle of blackberry wine, another of gin, and a third of a citrus liqueur. "Hopefully someone will think to bring good mixers." She handed one of the bottles to Hettie and then tucked one under each arm.

The butler eyed them askance when they asked for their coats as a black cab arrived in front.

"Don't worry, luv," Ro told the butler. "Your master doesn't mind."

None of them believed that whopper of a lie, but Ro's cheerful proclamation somehow made it acceptable.

"Thief," Hettie hissed innocently as the driver opened the door to the black cab. She dove inside. Struggling with the cork, she asked, "Are we going to the baths nude or shall we grab bathing costumes?"

"My brother-in-law lives with us," Ro said, looking disgusted. "I'll be going nude before I go back and face that one. Oh..." Her head cocked as the black cab sped up. "I think that's him!"

"I'm a bit too round to really want to go full starkers," Hettie said, uninterested in seeing the brother-in-law.

"The men love the curves," Ro told her. "If you wanted to step out on your Harvey, you'd just need to up the attitude and cast a come-hither gaze."

"Like this?" Hettie asked, attempting one but feeling as though she must look as though she had something in her eye.

"Like this," Ro countered, glancing at Hettie out of the corner of her eye. "I'm thinking of a scrumptious plate of biscuits."

Hettie tried it and Ro bit back a laugh. "Are you angry with the biscuits?"

"Let me try imagining cakes. I do prefer a lemon cake." Hettie glanced at Ro out of the corner of her eye, imagining a heavily-iced lemon cake, and then smiled just a little.

"No, no," Ro said, showing Hettie again what to do.

"Oh! I know." Hettie imagined the divorce act that the parliament was considering.

"Yes! Now you've got it! Was it a box of chocolates?"

Hettie confessed, sending Ro into a bout of laughter and tears that saw them all the way to Hettie's hotel. From her hotel room to Ro's rooms, there were random burst of giggles and stray tears. Once they reached to bath house, Ro said, "I'll be drinking to that divorce act tonight. Possibly for the rest of my life."

"If it frees me," Hettie told Ro dryly, "I'd paper my house with copies of it to celebrate those who saved us from a fate I should have known better than to fall into."

Order your copy here.

ALSO BY BETH BYERS

The Hettie and Ro Adventures

co-written with Bettie Jane

Philanderers Gone

Adventurer Gone

Holiday Gone

Aeronaut Gone

The Poison Ink Mysteries

Death By the Book

Death Witnessed

Death by Blackmail

Death Misconstrued

Deathly Ever After

The 2nd Chance Diner Mysteries

Spaghetti, Meatballs, & Murder

Cookies & Catastrophe

Poison & Pie

Double Mocha Murder

Cinnamon Rolls & Cyanide

Tea & Temptation

Donuts & Danger

Scones & Scandal

Lemonade & Loathing

Wedding Cake & Woe

Honeymoons & Honeydew

The Pumpkin Problem

ALSO BY AMANDA A. ALLEN

The Mystic Cove Mommy Mysteries

Bedtimes & Broomsticks

Runes & Roller Skates

Banshees and Babysitters

Hobgoblins and Homework

Christmas and Curses

Valentines & Valkyries

The Rue Hallow Mysteries

Hallow Graves

Hungry Graves

Lonely Graves

Sisters and Graves

Yule Graves

Fated Graves

Ruby Graves

The Inept Witches Mysteries

(co-written with Auburn Seal)

Inconvenient Murder

Moonlight Murder

Eastern
Revenue

2#5
J484
956 - 8681

Made in the USA
Middletown, DE
04 July 2021